# ACCIDENTAL RIVALS

## AN OFFICE ROMANCE

RIVER LAURENT

Other Books By River

Cinderella.com
Taken By The Baller
Daddy's Girl
Dear Neighbor
CEO & I
Dare Me
Kissing Booth
Single Dad
The Promise
Too Hot To Handle

978-1-911608-23-3

# ACKNOWLEDGMENTS

Many, many thanks to:
Leanore Eliott
Brittany Urbaniak
Peggy Schnurr

# SIENNA

There are people who drag their butts into the office on Monday morning, then spend the next five days looking forward to Friday evening.

I'm not one of them.

I don't just work Monday through Friday. Often, I'll work right through the weekend. And I freaking love it. I honestly do. I'm a career girl and I love my job. To me, work is such a huge part of my life that it is quite literally my whole life.

"Good morning," I greet, a bright smile plastered on my face as I breeze through the open floor plan layout of Dunhurst Real Estate. It reminds me of a beehive, so many cubicles attached to one another, so much buzzing among the worker bees.

One day, I'll have the corner office. I glance longingly at it every morning on my way to the cubicle-with-a-door which currently passes for my office. I suppose I should be grateful. At least, it has a door, and high walls to give me privacy. Most people don't even have that much.

I reach my door without getting pulled into random conversations about the weather, or questions about what I did during the weekend. That's always a pointless question, anyway. Everybody knows what I do with my time. I work. Maybe they're hoping I'll mix things up and talk about a great party, or recommend a movie I went to.

But how is a person supposed to hit their sales goals when they spend their weekends partying, going to brunch and the movies, or generally being slack? Whenever I overhear complaints from one of my coworkers about middling sales, I have to bite my tongue to keep from bringing this up.

If you want something great, you have to be willing to sacrifice the not-so-great stuff. It's all a matter of choices. Sure, I'd love to be able to maintain my position in the company while enjoying a busy social life, but that's not possible. It is what it is.

Closing my office door, I hang up my coat on the rack in the corner, and sit down to plan my day. Call me old-fashioned, but I believe in writing out my to-do lists at the start of every day. I can always add items to my ticker on the computer, but the act of writing it all down soothes me in a way technology simply can't. And it's an excuse to put down my phone for a minute.

A very, very rare minute for me.

"Call Cindy," I murmur, scrawling the name of one of my recently closed clients. I like to check in a week or so after closing to see how things are going with the new house, maybe send a gift basket or flowers. I add a sub-note beneath that to remind myself to place an order. I have other such calls to make after that, seeing as how I've sold four additional properties in the last month.

It's been busy. God, I love it.

A knock at my door makes my nose wrinkle. Can't they give me ten minutes of peace? "Yes?" I call out, forcing the irritation out of my voice.

Becca pokes her head in, her cloud of auburn curls making an appearance before she does. I wish I had hair as pretty as hers, but I know I'd never be able to get it to behave as well as hers. I'd probably end up a frizzy mess, forced to eternally wear a messy bun. Who has the time?

"Rodney's looking for you," she whispers before wincing.

My eyes dart over to my phone, checking the time. "Not even nine-fifteen yet? It must be my lucky day."

"Godspeed." She hurries off, probably grateful she's not the one the boss wants to see this early on a Monday.

I can only imagine what he wants from me at this time of the morning.

Rodney's not bad, as far as bosses go. I worked for some real winners throughout college, during my internship and in the year following that. Rodney's intense, sure, and a hard worker, I mean, how else would he get to be in the corner office? But he rewards good work and doles out opportunities to those he knows will make the most of them.

I hope that's what this is about.

I take a quick look at myself in my compact. My chocolate-brown hair is in place, smoothed back in its low ponytail. I really do wish I had more time to make it look nicer, but even when I try, it never comes out the way I'd like. The makeup around my hazel eyes looks good. I didn't smudge it on the way here.

I stand and smooth down the skirt of my black dress before striding out into the beehive. This could be good. No, this *will* be good. He's going to congratulate me on my sales last month. He's going to give me a raise. He's going to give me a new listing. He's going to…

The sight of an unwelcome presence outside his office door nearly stops me in my tracks.

U *gh.* Zack?

He would have to stop in for a moment of the boss's time when I'm on my way in for something I've decided must be very, very important. This is so like him, acting as if the entire world revolves around him and what he wants. Forget the rest of us, forget having a little consideration of his boss's time first thing on a Monday.

The thing is, he acts that way because people treat him as though it's okay to be an inconsiderate jerk. Just because he's good looking, the women around the office fawn over him like he's the second coming. I guess that sort of drop dead gorgeousness will breed confidence throughout other areas of life too. Not that I'm ugly or anything, just that he's in a class by himself. Even I can admit that, and I can't stand the man.

Why?

Because he's almost as good as me. Maybe as good as, certainly not better than. To date, he is my only competition in the company. The only agent who closes nearly as many properties as I do, for around as much money as I do.

All right. He had a slightly higher sales figure than I did last month, but only by a few measly hundred thousand dollars. That's nothing when you're selling the sort of luxury properties we handle.

Damn it, he's making a move to close Rodney's office door behind him. I put on a little speed, hurrying the rest of the way in order to catch the door before it swings shut.

"Excuse me," I murmur through gritted teeth. "I was told Rodney wanted to see me."

His ice blue eyes size me up, and one corner of his mouth quirks up in a smile. "Small world. So was I."

We both turn to our boss, who's seated behind his desk. As always, the office is pristine, without so much as a single paper or pen out of place. Not a single speck of dust anywhere. He's a very deliberate man, Rodney is.

If this were my office, I would be the same way.

He flashes us one of his million-dollar smiles, the sort of smile I'm still working on, the one that closes never ending, multi-million-dollar sales. "I wanted to see the both of you at once, as a matter of fact. Please, close the door and have a seat."

I exchange a look with Zack—for once, the two of us are in the same boat, both slightly confused and feeling as though we're about to go up in front of a firing squad. But if he can be confident, so can I. I close the door and walk over to one of the chairs facing Rodney's side of the desk, taking a seat and folding my hands in my lap.

He hasn't stopped smiling, looking for all the world like the cat that ate the canary. He has News for us, the sort of news that requires a capital-N when I imagine it in my head. I've seen that gleam in his eyes before. And it wasn't good the last time.

"We don't have much time, so I'll give you the Reader's Digest version: Nick McMann is selling his estate, and he's going with Dunhurst for the sale."

My mind immediately starts to race. The McMann property is legendary, built with the sort of money only a multi-platinum selling recording artist can afford to spend. I can see it in my head. It looks like something from that old TV show, *Dynasty*, somewhat more modern, but just as sprawling and over-the-top.

And he's going with us to close the sale.

I have a feeling I know why Rodney called us in, and I'm more than up to the challenge. He wants to see which of the two of us can close it first. No freaking contest. I already have a half-dozen people in mind to call up and see if they're interested.

A quick glance out of the corner of my eye tells me Zack's thinking along the same lines. He can't hide that wolfish smile he gets on his stupid face whenever he sees himself close to a big sale. I wonder how he manages to sell anything at all, seeing as how he gives away what he's thinking with that stupid, arrogant smile of his.

I'm gonna wipe the floor with him.

"We're talking the sale of the decade here," Rodney continues, oblivious to the silent war going on between his staff. As far as he's concerned, Zack and I are his two shining stars. I don't think he would care even if he knew we hated each other, so long as we keep making money for the company.

"No kidding," Zack observes with a smarmy grin.

God, he is such an ass kisser.

"There's just one little catch." Rodney's smile fades. "It has to be closed within a week."

"What?" I realize a moment later that Zack said it just as I did.

For once, something has managed to knock him off his high horse. He looks just as shook as I feel.

Rodney holds up his hands, signaling silence before the two of us can continue to work ourselves into a frenzy.

A week? Is he insane?

"It's the only stipulation Nick has. He wants the sale finalized in a week. He's moving out of the country and doesn't want any loose ends."

"A week? He's crazy," I mutter. Just like a clueless celebrity. He obviously doesn't understand or doesn't care about how much work goes into a sale, especially a high-profile sale like this one. They think we can just snap our fingers and make magic happen.

"If there's anyone I trust to get this done, it's the two of you."

Silence. He is greeted by complete silence for at least five seconds after dropping that adorable little bombshell on our heads. I'm still reeling from the timeline situation, and he goes and adds this to the mix.

"The two of us?" Zack croaks.

I can't help but feel slightly pleased at his incredulity, even though I know it comes from the fact that he likes me around him as much as I like to be around him. Which is to say—not even a little bit.

Meanwhile, I'm too gob smacked to speak. What is there to say? To argue with him would make me look childish, and I know Rodney well enough by now to know he doesn't change his mind once he's made it up. I can only sit here and absorb whatever it is he has to say.

"The two of you," he confirms, smiling again. "You're the two best salespeople I have, which shouldn't be a surprise to either of you. I couldn't trust anyone, but you guys to do this. Let's face it… this will be a challenge, and a big one so I would rather have two great minds on it rather than only one. And considering the price Nick's looking to pull down, your commission will be sizable even when split in half."

Zack looks like somebody just killed his dog.

I feel like somebody just killed mine. If I had one, that is. This isn't going to go well. I can't believe Rodney would do this—high-profile sale or not. The fact that he doesn't have enough faith in me to let me handle it on my own speaks volumes. I'm not a child. I don't need my hand held.

And I sure as hell don't need Zack sliming his way around the place, doing little work and taking all the credit for what's surely going to be my sale. I've never exactly had a lot of respect for people who charm their way through life without actually working for anything, which is exactly the sort of guy he is.

"Off you go, then. You both have a lot of work to do. Becca should have all the preliminary information together for you by now."

When he turns to face his laptop, I know we've been dismissed for good. No chance of changing his mind, no way to beg him to reconsider without looking like a whiny little crybaby.

My knees are shaking as I stand, but I do my best to cover up the absolute fury roiling in my stomach as I walk out with Zack behind me. There are times when even the biggest sale and tastiest commission isn't worth it. I hope this isn't one of those times, but something tells me it will be.

No wonder people hate Mondays so much. I think I might start hating them, too.

## ZACK

He's got to be kidding. Even as I walk out of the door I keep waiting for him to yell "Gotcha!" or something like that, but he hasn't. Yet. I'm afraid he never will. I'm afraid he seriously means to pair us together.

*Her?* He wants me to work with the ice princess? Doesn't he know what an insufferable little bitch she is? And that's not me being mean. Hell, everybody in the office thinks so. They're just too afraid of her, and of the way Rodney obviously loves her, to say anything about it. She's one of the two top agents in the company.

I just happen to be the other one.

If Rodney wasn't such a stickler for keeping everybody accountable by making us work like bees in a hive, there would be three offices on our floor instead of only his. Mine would be one of them, and hers would be the other one. Even I can admit she's damn good at what she does.

Why does she have to be such a hard-nosed bitch about it, though? That's what I don't get. All she cares about is work, all she wants is the sale. Forget making friends in the office, forget being a human being and not some robot who understands nothing but numbers and commissions. There isn't even any making small talk with her. She can't even be bothered to take time out of her busy day around the coffee maker, the way civilized people do when they work together.

There's a reason I steer clear of her and anybody like her, male or female. Especially when they happen to be my competition.

Now, Rodney has gone and dropped her in my fucking lap and asked me to play nice. We have to be a team. I've never been good at acting as though I like someone when I don't. And I don't have a reputation for playing nice.

What a hell of a week this is going to be.

I follow her out of Rodney's office and wish she wasn't wearing that tight dress. It's not enough that I have to work with her. I have to watch that cute little ass wiggling back and forth every time she walks past.

I know I don't technically have to watch. I just can't help it. Why does she have to be so… her?

It's not like I've ever had trouble with women—far from it. Even now, I catch three passing coworkers checking me out. I'm used to it. I'm not being big-headed. It's just a fact of life. If I decided I wanted a little company tonight, it wouldn't be too hard to convince any of the single women in the office to join me.

My gaze drops to the straight set of shoulders marching ahead of me. But this one. This Sienna. She acts like she's untouchable, like she has no time for anything as basic as sexual needs. She's so far above mere mortals like me. That's probably my biggest problem with her.

We reach her wannabe office first, as mine is at the other end of the floor. Thank God, I'm not checking her ass out anymore when she stops suddenly and turns around to glare at me. I don't need her accusing me of harassment.

She sighs, like she's the only one with a problem.

I barely manage to hold my tongue to keep from asking if I'm making her late for the surgery to get the stick removed from her ass.

"I guess we should take some time to go over a plan for this," she says, making sure to sound as bored as possible.

"Yes, I guess so. I should be able to clear some time today."

Her eyes roll. It's clearly a gesture she's practiced throughout her life. "Dinner tonight. I'll send you a calendar request. We can talk it over then."

"I can hardly wait."

She rewards me with another eye roll before stepping into her makeshift office and closing the door with a decisive snap of the latch.

She'd better not plan on acting that way throughout our time together, but something tells me she will. She'll make me feel like this is the ultimate inconvenience. Like she's supremely put out by this. She has to be the most self-centered person I've ever met.

Which is saying something, because I've known my share. Without warning, completely and inappropriately, an image of her sour mouth wrapped around my cock slips into my head. Immediately, my cock twitches with interest.

Fuck!

I jam my fists into my pants pockets and continue to my desk, grateful she can't see the way she's affected me. It would be a power trip for her to know I'm secretly lusting after her. Which is extremely annoying.

She'd better not plan on continuing to act that way throughout our time together, but something tells me she will. She'll treat me like this is the ultimate inconvenience, like she's supremely put out by this, because she's the most self-centered person I've ever met.

Which is saying something, because I've known my share.

I jam my fists into my pants pockets before continuing to my desk, grateful that she can't see the way she's unnerved me. I don't usually react to women like this and I don't like showing my hand so easily... not to someone like Sienna. How am I supposed to rush through this job and still do it the right way when she's a part of it?

At least I have a door to close behind me, shutting out the rest of the office for a while. They don't need to see me sitting there with my head in my hands. It would ruin the image I've put together over the years.

I guess I have no choice. I can't refuse Rodney. I need this sale. Not for the commission. She's welcome to it all if she'll just let me take the credit for it. I have my reasons for needing this sale on my resume and it's nothing to do with money. Worst part is, I know I could close this sale on my own. No point asking her to let me make the sale on my own in exchange for all the commission. Knowing the way she is, she'll want to take all the credit, all the commission, and my head on a platter.

There's got to be a way to get around her.

An idea starts to bloom in my mind, one which probably isn't completely fair, but hey, all's fair in love and war and real estate. I don't feel too bad about it, as I'll let her keep all the commission.

Anyway, instinct tells me she'd do the same to me if she had enough imagination.

## SIENNA

So…here I am. Doing something, I thought I'd never do —have dinner with one of my coworkers in a fairly intimate, romantic restaurant. The fact that it's Zack sitting across from me doesn't make me feel any more comfortable with the situation. If anything, it just about turns my stomach.

I've been trying all day to figure out just what it is that makes me dislike him so much. It's more than competition, since I've been a competitive person since the day I was born. I'm not the type to begrudge others their success, either. That's petty, and I'm not a petty person.

It's like he brings out every single one of my worst qualities, qualities I would rather pretend aren't there. Why would I want to spend time with a person who does that to me? I tell myself it's all right then, to wish this dinner were over.

Even though we've barely begun.

"How's your wine?" he asks, nodding at my mostly-full glass.

"Very nice," I murmur distantly, observing the easy way he sits so casually in his chair while making it look as though he's posing for a magazine ad. Men's suits or luxury watches, something like that, or maybe a high-priced liquor. He's removed his tie and the first two buttons of his starched white shirt are open to reveal a tanned throat leading to what I can only imagine is a tanned chest.

Oh, my God. I can't believe that thought crossed my mind. I just need more wine.

No, on second thought. Anything but that. Maybe a cold shower. Shame, they don't offer those at the restaurant.

His icy eyes are more striking than ever in the candlelight. What was I thinking, picking a place with candles on the tables? But who thinks to check on things like that when they're making a reservation? And how was I supposed to know I would care? I look away and catch a woman watching me. She seems, well, envious. I look away quickly. Oh dear, everybody here probably thinks we're a couple. This is such a joke.

"Feeling any better about the listing?" he asks, sipping his Scotch.

I frown, waiting for him to elaborate. When he doesn't I dive in, "Who says I didn't already feel good about it?"

"Oh, come on." He grins, shaking his head. "Let's put our cards on the table, shall we?"

"By all means," I agree, leaning slightly forward.

"We both know it's going to be difficult, if not impossible, to share this listing. Neither of us takes well to teamwork. That's not criticism," he adds, speaking quickly when he sees my eyes widen at his words. "I'm speaking for both of us right now. I know how I am, and I'm not keen on sharing the glory. I can only imagine you feel the same way, considering the record you have with the company. We're the cream of the crop." He lifts his glass ever so slightly, as though to toast me.

I return the gesture. For once, we're being honest with each other. "Your record is impressive," I allow, still eyeing him up. What's he getting at?

"Thank you." He returns the glass to the table and folds his hands. "With that being said, I think there's only one cut-and-dried solution to the situation in which we've found ourselves."

"Oh? I'm all ears."

His smile widens.

Uh-oh. There's the wolf I saw this morning. He's trying to steer me in the direction he wants this to go. I steel myself for what's about to come out of his mouth—though there's no way I could have predicted just how ridiculous it would be.

"This will go much easier for both of us if you agree to step down and give me the listing. In return, I'll guarantee that you can keep the whole commission."

And the way he says it! As though he expects me to go for it? I think that's the most surprising part of all.

I blink. Hard. More than once. He's not a stupid man, not by a long shot. Why, then, would he believe it would be so easy to steamroll me? Unless he's joking. But when he doesn't say anything to make me think he was kidding, a laugh bubbles out of my throat. It comes out before I can stop it.

And it's enough to knock his wolfish smile crooked.

Good.

"You're not serious. Please, tell me you're not serious." I say when I manage to calm myself down before I end up making a scene.

"Of course, I am. I wouldn't joke about something this important."

Looking at his unamused face I take a long swig of my wine. I'm going to need to fortify myself if this is the way the night is going to go. "All right, then." I put down the glass and sit up straighter in my chair. If he wants to play, we can play. "Let's get this out of the way right now: I will not be stepping down. I will not request another listing. While your offer of the entire commission is very attractive, I think I'll pass since I want the glory just as much as you do. While I have to admit I'm not thrilled to pieces over the idea of our working together, that's just the way this unfolded. We don't have much time to get it done, and it has to be done right. So let's spare each other and stop wasting time talking about things which will never happen. All right?"

It's his turn to blink and look surprised by my forthrightness.

I get the feeling he's not used to being challenged or refused. Is there actually a world in which he'd make a statement like that and get his way? There must be, or else he would allow my laughter to roll off his back instead of appearing so genuinely shocked that I turned him down.

No wonder he walks around with his nose in the air.

Nobody's ever challenged him before. He's in for a wake-up, if that's the case.

He shakes his head ever so slightly, as though he's shaking off the setback, then smiles again, but this time, he looks a bit sheepish. "You can't blame me for trying, can you?"

Mr. Charming, I note to myself. Is this his new tactic? "No, I guess I can't," I allow, watching him closely.

"Right, might as well get down to some work then," he says evenly.

Is he really going to give up that easily? I don't think so. Even so, we manage to get some work done. He appears to buckle down when discussing the strategy we should put in place. I have to admit, he knows his stuff. I've wondered in the back of my mind for a long time whether his success was based solely on his looks and charm. It can't be an accident that most of his biggest sales have involved women.

If anything, that would've been a comfort, blaming his excellent record on a fluke; the fact that he happens to be born handsome. Not so. He's a smart guy, cunning too, and a hard worker. Sometimes, I see him leave at the same time I do. Damn it. I don't want to admire him.

"I'll call up the photographer and set up a photo shoot for tomorrow afternoon. Then we can get the listing up tomorrow and start rolling," he suggests.

"So long as you can guarantee your guy will take the best photos possible, because we could always use my go-to."

"I take it you've never seen any of my listings," he says with a smirk.

"Oh, I have." Have I ever. Why wouldn't I look over the work of my rival? And yes, that's how I see him, even if we work for the same company. "And I'm telling you, I hope you can vouch for the quality of these pictures."

His laughter surprises me—and from the look on his face, it surprises him as well. "Touché. But not to worry. We'll present it like the showplace it is."

"Good." I can't help but smile a little as I raise the wine glass to my lips. It's a relief to know we're on the same page, for the most part, and moving forward.

The food arrives, and at the right time too. We were about to hit one of those awkward silences. He smiles charmingly at the waitress and I have to wonder about him. What's he all about? I'd rather boil myself in oil than dare ask. I still don't trust him, and I wouldn't put it past him to take my curiosity as a sign of something deeper.

But he seems just as curious about me too. "So what drives you to be as good as you are?" he asks, flashing that winning smile.

It surprises me that he doesn't bother to disguise his interest, though. I'd rather die than let him know that I secretly find him distractingly attractive. I clear my throat before speaking, "I've always been an overachiever, before I even knew what the word meant," I admit, thinking back to my days in elementary school. "For as long as I can remember, I was that nerdy kid who asked for extra credit work, just to boost my grade. I mean, if I could get all A's, why not try for a solid row of A+?"

He chuckles, stroking his square chin.

It's the sort of chin I have always wanted to punch or run my fingers down. Damn. Where did that come from? I pick up my glass, take a huge swallow, and nearly choke.

"Are you all right?"

I feel my cheeks heat up as I wave his question away. I bet he would love it if I choked and died right here. "Fine. I'm fine."

"I guess I was much the same way as you," he admits, picking up his knife and fork. "Looking back, I guess I was pretty insufferable."

*You're pretty insufferable now.* Fortunately, that thought remains a silent one in my head. "So you get where I'm coming from."

"Better than you know." He grins. "It doesn't surprise me, though."

My fork stills on the way to my mouth. "What doesn't surprise you?" I ask suspiciously.

He shakes his head. "How alike we were from the start. There had to be a reason why you caught my attention. And not just because you're such a star in the office, either."

Darn him. I feel the heat burn up from my throat into my cheeks and all over my chest. It has to be the wine. Red wine always does this to me. *Quick... say something to cover the obvious innuendo.* "Funny. I thought I would've caught your attention because I outsold you last year."

"Ouch." He's smirking as he raises his glass to his lips, holding my gaze over the rim.

I wish I could stop grinning. But then again, he's smiling, so I am. Why be mean or nasty? There's no need to be. "Flattery will get you nowhere," I warn, but I'm still sort of smiling, so the weight of my message is inevitably lost.

"We'll see. I've found that flattery, when used correctly, can at least get one's foot in the door. What a person chooses to do once their foot's in the door, well…that depends on the skill of the person we're talking about." He shrugs, one eyebrow raised, as he butters his roll.

God, he has really nice hands. Big, and capable and I love men with strong wrists. The black strap of his watch peeks out of his sleeve. Very sexy.

Wait. What's happening right now? Unbeknownst to me my whole posture has changed. I'm leaning forward in a relaxed way and maybe even enjoying the conversation. This isn't what I'd planned on. I don't need to enjoy his company. In fact, that's the worst thing I can do, because it's just a hop, skip and a jump from there to falling under his spell.

He's doing this on purpose, isn't he?

I eye him up as I chew slowly, glad to have the chance to get my hormones in check. Yes, he's definitely more friendly and personable than he'd acted earlier, and much more so than he's ever been before. Plenty of grins, jokes, and more than a little bit of flirting.

It's been a long time since I've been flirted with, but I remember how it goes.

I can't believe he almost reeled me in, the snake.

"What would you say to dessert?" he asks, offering a smooth smile. "We could always share something really wicked, if you want to. You don't look like you overindulge."

Instead of answering, I wipe the corners of my mouth with my napkin and signal for the check. "I would appreciate it if you didn't comment on my body or dining choices," I inform him while looking for my wallet.

"Excuse me?"

"You heard me," I reply in a clipped and businesslike tone. "I didn't ask for your opinion on my body, or whether or not it looks as though I make a habit of overindulging. So, please. Let's keep this professional."

"I don't understand," he insists, all innocence. "What happened? I thought we were having a nice time, for once."

"We were." Maybe a little too good of a time. Maybe that was exactly what he's been counting on, getting me to loosen up and fall under his spell, so he can pounce on the listing and leave me in the dust. There's no other explanation for his sudden change of heart. He went from telling me to leave the listing alone to telling me he likes my body, for all intents and purposes.

"What happened?" he asks again.

Instead of telling him I'm on to his game, I shrug it off. "I remembered I have a lot of work to do when I get home... and you do too, no doubt," I add on handing my card over. "You have to call that photographer."

"Wait a second." He reaches for his wallet.

I signal for him to stop. "Don't worry about dinner," I murmur.

He's overwhelmed, flabbergasted, struggling to catch up as I stand with my purse, intent on following the server to the register. The sooner this is over, the better. I pass him by without another look. I wouldn't accept a meal from that snake for anything. Not even this listing all to myself. I wouldn't want to be in his debt.

The creep.

# SIENNA

I wake up the next morning, as I normally do... surrounded by work. I must've fallen asleep with the laptop open beside me, the phone next to my pillow. I was up until late in the night, sending emails to any contacts who could come through with leads on a buyer. They're used to getting these messages from me at all hours of the morning, but it's not as if I don't keep our relationship warm outside of asking for favors. I scratch their backs whenever I can too.

It takes a second for the fog to clear, and then I realize what woke me. The buzzing of my phone, signaling a text. The thin beams of light coming in through the mostly-drawn drapes tells me I've slept a little later than usual. That one glass of wine sure did me in. Sure enough, on picking up the phone I find that it's past eight. Practically unheard of for me.

*Where are you? Photographer's here, as is Nick. Just waiting on you.*

Wait. What? I have to read Zack's text again to be sure I'm not imagining things. Is this a bad dream? No way is he texting me with this right now. It's like I'm having a nightmare where I'm back at school and someone is telling me I've missed a big exam I've been cramming for has come and gone. I still have those 'slept right through it all' nightmares to this day.

But…no such luck this morning. I'm most definitely awake, and he's most definitely telling me that I'm in bed while he's waiting on me at the property. With our seller.

I can't text him back when it's something as important as this.

He answers on the first ring. "Well? Where are you?"

"I don't understand," I say, keeping my voice as calm as I can while I race through the bedroom at breakneck speed, the phone on speaker so I can talk and prepare. "You told me you would set this up for the afternoon."

A pause. "No, I didn't."

"Yes, you most certainly did," I hiss as I run a brush through my hair. "You said it would be this afternoon. You were going to call the photographer yet and set it up for the afternoon."

"You must have misheard," he retorts. "Anyway, don't sweat it if you can't be here for this. I'll take care of it."

"Oh, no, no, no," I assure him, sliding into a dress and zipping as I jam my feet into pumps. "I'll be there in ten minutes."

Another pause—longer, this time. "You're sure?"

"Absolutely. See you then." The moment I'm certain the call is over and he can't hear, I let loose a string of curses the likes of which haven't left my mouth since the last time I got good and drunk after losing a big deal. That son of a bitch. Who does he think he's playing with?

It's a ten-minute drive on a good day in light traffic. I make it in seven, pulling to a stop in front of the magnificent lake-front estate with a tight smile for Zack, who's waiting for me out front.

"That was a quick drive. You couldn't have been very far away," he comments, looking as cool and suave as ever. A wayward breeze plays at his hair and he reaches up to swipe it away from his sparkling eyes.

Damn him. He looks just as alluring as he did at dinner last night. Maybe even more. And I thought it was just the lights and the wine. I quickly avert my gaze from his and close the car door without slamming it. I take a deep breath then let him have it, "What's the game here, Zack?" I ask in a tight whisper as I stalk up to him.

"What do you mean, game?" Oh, his eyes are so wide and innocent.

I wonder how one of them would look after I punch it. He might have a good half-foot on me even when I'm wearing heels, but I've been taking kickboxing classes for years and would love the opportunity to practice on him. "I mean I know for certain that we talked about doing this in the afternoon. You said you hadn't even called him yet last night, for Christ's sake." I narrow my eyes. "Either you set this up before last night or you pulled some strings to get it arranged so fast."

He crosses his arms. "I pulled some strings."

"You could've called or texted to let me know," I say, not fully convinced that he was telling the truth.

"I told you at dinner it would be first thing this morning. I'm sorry if a glass of wine makes you a little forgetful." He shrugs, unable to keep a tiny little smirk at bay.

Forget giving him a black eye. I'm gonna rip his throat out.

He's saved by the opening of the door and the appearance of none other than Nick McCann, looking every bit as disheveled and absent-minded as he does during interviews and appearances. It's his shtick, I guess, but I've never been able to decide if he's cute or not. He's just got one of those laid back personalities that I'm sure would drive me crazy after a week.

He comes out with one hand extended, an almost apologetic smile on his offbeat face. "Sorry for the confusion," he says. "Your man here tells me there was a misunderstanding?"

"We're not together," we announce simultaneously.

Nick smiles slowly.

Now it takes all the self-control in my body to keep from blushing and looking away. Boy, we must really come off as amateurs.

I take a deep breath. So Zack thinks he's charming? Well, he's never seen me in action. I flash Nick my widest, most ingratiating smile while returning his handshake with a firm, no-nonsense grip of my own. I can tell from the way his eyebrows quirk up that he didn't expect it.

"Why don't you show me around this magnificent place?" I

ask. "What a pleasure it is, helping put an estate like this on the market."

"Oh, yes?" he asks, leading the way with a sweep of his arm.

"Please?" I giggle, sweeping my hair over one shoulder as we walk, not bothering to throw a glance Zack's way. "A show-place such as this will practically sell itself. No sweat."

# SIENNA

I wonder how Rodney will feel about me killing Zack and disposing of his body in a vat of acid. He's probably the only one who would care. No way this idiot has anybody who loves him.

At least we got the pictures and dimensions of every room, which took a long while considering the number of rooms involved, but it gave me a chance to work on Nick. By the time I finished, he was suitably impressed with my system for taking measurements, the laser I used to capture the room's dimensions and the program which I fed the information into that automatically created a layout on my tablet.

It becomes clear Zack is fuming no matter how hard he works at hiding it.

Nick might have been fooled, but not me. I've seen that expression on his face before. Like he's eaten something he wishes he hadn't. Still, better whatever it was than my fist, which is what he almost ate after pulling such a nasty trick on me.

It backfired, since I'm only more determined than ever to cozy up to Nick and earn his trust.

Now he knows who he's dealing with.

"I'll write up the listing," I announce as I stride into my cubicle, not bothering to wait for his reply before closing the door. I got the last word. That counts for something, and it also means I don't have to rely on him for anything, since I know I can't trust him.

Besides, it means I don't have to give him the satisfaction of working on it with me.

I've been in the game for nearly five solid years now, and I've never been one to rely on an assistant to help me prepare something so critical to the success of a property. All the normal buzzwords run through my head as I get to work. Spacious, luxury, breathtaking, sweeping views.

When my phone goes off, I'm almost certain without looking over that it's Zack calling, trying to mess with my flow, but it's not. I smile the first real, genuine smile of the day when I see my sister's name on the screen. "Tami, you know I don't usually have time to take calls at work," I say with a little chuckle.

"Oh, I'm sorry," she gushes breathlessly, completely sarcastic. "I forgot I'm only allowed to call during the three-point-four minutes per day you're not actually working."

"Whoa, whoa." I laugh. "It's at least five-and-a-half, exaggerator. What's up?"

Her heavy sigh tells me it's exactly what I thought it would be. I'm used to these calls, which come around once or twice a week now. When she first got engaged, it was more like once every two weeks. I'm sure that by the time the big day comes along, she'll be calling on the hour.

"I did try not to call you, but I'm so freaking stressed about the flowers. Do you think the florist will be able to get their hands on enough hydrangeas, what with this unseasonably cool weather?"

It's always best to take a calm, reasonable approach with her when she gets this way. I keep my voice low and soothing, just the way she needs it to be. "I'm sure they'll be able to handle it," I murmur, sitting back in my chair with my eyes closed. I need a brief break from the stress in my life right now, anyway. And for some strange reason, soothing my sister actually soothes me too.

"You think so?"

"Sweetheart, any florist worth the money is going to have backup vendors in place. I'm sure they can call in reinforcements if there are any issues with quantity, or even quality. We researched for a solid month before deciding on these girls, and I've still heard nothing but rave reviews about them since then."

"You mean it?" She sounds hopeful again.

"Of course. I keep my eyes open for stuff like this. You know I do. It's the Maid of Honor's responsibility, isn't it?"

"You're right. I should know better by now than to second-guess you." Her tone brightens instantly.

I have to wonder if she wakes up every morning with another random worry sitting at the forefront of her thoughts. If that's the case, it's a miracle she's managed to hold on to her sanity for this long—and that's saying something, because she's driving herself crazy, examining every possible thing that could go wrong.

Is this really what getting married is like, I'm glad to be single.

Then again, Tami's always been on the high-strung side, while I'm practical and level-headed. Maybe something like a wedding just brings out a bride's personality, or maybe every bride goes a bit crazy over what we're told from the time we're little girls is the 'Biggest, Best Day Of Our Life.'

Once she's away from the ledge and feeling better, I hang up and get back to the listing. I wasn't making it up when I told Nick a home like his could sell itself. The location, right there on the lake. The sheer size. The wide-open feeling of it, each room flowing into the next. The massive wine cellar, the media room with its theater seating, surround sound and wall-sized screen. The library, which Nick currently uses as a music room, but could easily become an office or even a family room. A dining room that can seat thirty with no problem.

It's a showplace, a jewel.

On the other hand, it's perfect for a wealthy family too. There's a chef's kitchen with an intimate little breakfast nook. Smaller bedrooms just perfect for children, with a separate bathroom for each. Lots of room outdoors to run and play, and a dock which leads out to the water. I can imagine a sailboat tied off there, waiting for a family to take it out on a beautiful day. No matter who the buyer is, no matter their lifestyle, they'll find what they're looking for in that house.

I put it all in the listing and then some. After a solid hour of tinkering with it, I sit back, happy with the finished product. A very tiny, miniscule part of me wonders if I'm doing the right thing by not running this past Zack before posting it on our website, but I quickly remind myself there's no doubt that he would do it to me in a heartbeat.

Look how he tried to muscle me out of the meeting with Nick today.

I click the "Publish" button with relish.

Now that the listing is live, I can start making phone calls. I can't help but notice the way my heart races a little, as I start going through my contacts and the latest notes I've made on each of them. This is the part I like best - pairing a contact with the home I know is perfect for them - knowing I was right when things line up and I close the deal.

My eyes widen when I come to Mark's name. Hmm. Is it worth giving him a call? I know he's always claimed to be in the market for a high worth lakeside home. He could afford it. And this is probably the most highly-coveted location in the area.

It's worth a try, but is it worth opening a can of worms over?

I chew my lip, tapping my fingers on the desk, questioning myself. It's been over a year since we broke up, maybe longer than that. I didn't exactly circle the date in red on my calendar. Can I handle hanging out with Mark?

Certainly. He's a good guy, we always got along and it's not as if we ended things bitterly, either. It just didn't work out. No big surprise, one of the major issues had to do with my work habits. He wanted a woman who would jump when he snapped his fingers, who'd drop everything for him and I couldn't be that person. All it did was cause us both grief, until I did the decent thing and ended it.

It was over well before that, though and with time, he should have seen that too.

Who knows? He might actually be glad to hear from me. Stranger things have happened. I haven't heard anything about him being involved with another woman yet, either, but that has nothing to do with this. My fingers are already on the dial buttons. Strangely, I still remember his number by heart.

He sounds surprised to hear from me, but not unhappy. "What a surprise! What have you been up to?" he asks before chuckling. "Wait, let me guess. You've been working."

I dig the nails of one hand into my palm and force a chuckle of my own. What's he going to say when he finds out that this call is about that very thing? "Wow. You know me too well."

"I'm waiting for the day when you tell me there's something more than that going on in your life, beautiful." He sounds kind and warm, like a friend. No judgment.

"It's funny you should mention work…"

"Uh-oh."

"No, this is a good thing. I just had a new property land in my lap and I thought of you." I can't help but feel another twinge of conscience on delivering this line, but I remind myself again, that Zack would do this to me in a heartbeat. If anything, it'll serve him right.

The fact is, if I make this sale to one of my contacts, everyone will know I was the one responsible. The same would be true if it was one of Zack's friends, or exes. Not that I would expect him to have an ex-girlfriend. That would mean first finding a woman who could put up with him, which I can't imagine.

I have to get this sale. For me. Just to prove myself, if nothing else.

We decide on dinner later in the evening, and a private tour of the house afterward. Nick's officially moved out now, so there's no reason why we shouldn't take a look.

Without Zack knowing.

We'll see how he likes it.

## SIENNA

"You are going to lose your mind over this place," I promise as I unlock the door.

"Oh, yeah?"

"Absolutely. I saw the kitchen and immediately thought about you making brunch at the stove. I still remember those crepes you made that one day."

"Definitely the peak of my brunch career." He chuckles as we step into the two-story foyer with its marble floors and sweeping double staircase that meets in the center at a balcony which overlooks the space, then extends into a hallway in both directions.

That, and the terrible, awful, nauseating stench.

"Oh, my God," I groan, throwing my hands over my nose and mouth. The grilled chicken salad I just enjoyed for dinner threatens to come back up for a second visit.

"What the hell is that?" Mark chokes, waving his hands in

front of his face as though that will do anything to clear the air.

"I have no idea," I reply before gagging. "Oh, lord, it's terrible. I swear, it didn't smell anything like this earlier today. I was literally just here this morning for photos and everything was fine." I immediately rush to the kitchen, thinking the drain backed up.

"What about the bathrooms?" Mark asks, referencing the obvious nature of the smell.

I unlock the French doors and slide them wide open. I swear, I'll die if it's the toilets. How are we supposed to sell a home with crappy plumbing, no pun intended? "Hang out here and enjoy the view while I figure out what is going on."

"Nah, I'll help you look," Mark says joining me on the terrace.

Once I confirm it isn't the kitchen or garbage disposal, I take a chance on one of the first-floor bathrooms. Then another. Both of them appear to be fine, but the stench hasn't dissipated any.

"I'll open some windows," Mark offers, going to the first set he finds and flinging them open.

The fresh air helps, but not enough.

"This is so embarrassing," I mutter as I go from room to room, my hand still over my mouth and nose. It's not helping. What the heck happened here? Whatever it was, it happened fast. "I'm sorry. I would never have brought you here if I had any idea, obviously."

"Hey, things happen." He sounds way too relaxed, considering the situation we're in. Then again, it's not his listing on the line here. He can afford to be chill, to follow me from room to room, as I search in vain for the source of the stench.

Thank God, it doesn't seem to be coming from any of the bathrooms. They're all immaculate. The smell seems to be clearing up thanks to the open windows. After running the entire length and breadth of the house in a pair of four-inch heels, I'm exhausted, but not beaten.

"Well, here she is," I say with bright laugh, spreading my arms open when we're back in the foyer. "A bit of a quick tour, I admit, but you got a look at every single room."

"Bathrooms included." His brown eyes sparkle with good-natured laughter as he turns in a slow circle, looking up at the chandelier hanging in the center of the foyer. "And I have to admit, it's spectacular, Sienna. It's funny that you should remember how much I've always wanted to own a home out here."

I grin. "That's my job, remembering things like that."

He looks at me, frowning a little. "Funny. I was hoping you'd say you remembered because I said it."

"Oh, Mark…" To my horror, I start to blush. It's like we're reliving all those old memories, all the times he made me feel like I was coming up short because I didn't take something the way he wanted me to. And I did come up short, I'm fully aware. I wasn't the girlfriend he wanted or deserved. But that doesn't mean I need a guilt trip down Memory Lane.

He holds up his hands, feigning surrender. "Sorry, sorry. Couldn't help it."

"You know how rotten I feel about what happened."

"I know." He comes to me, a slight smile taking the place of the frown. "And I was hoping tonight could sort of—I don't know—help smooth things over a little."

Wait. What? His hands land on my waist. Not demanding or anything, but definitely a little more possessive than an ex has any right to be.

"I don't think we're quite on the same page, Mark." I place my hands over his—gentle, but determined. He's lucky I don't consider him a threat, or else he'd get a face full of the pepper spray I carry in my purse. If he thought what we were smelling earlier was bad…

"What do you mean, not on the same page? I thought we had a good time tonight." He knows I'm a sucker for his smile, especially when he's being sort of roguish. Like right now.

"We did. Dinner was really nice. I'm glad we got the chance to catch up and I'm glad things are going well for you." Very firmly, I remove his hands from my waist and hold them in mine, more to keep him from pawing me again than anything else. "But I don't want to give you the wrong idea. I didn't ask to see you tonight because I wanted to—well, you know…"

His eyes darken. "You didn't want me to get the idea that you actually wanted to see me for myself. Is that it? This is all business to you, the way everything always is."

"That's not fair."

"Isn't it? All you ever cared about was your next sale, your next commission, how your numbers would stack up against the rest of the company. It didn't matter what I wanted."

I can't help wanting to ask him why he'd think I'd give half a damn what he wants now if I was such a raging bitch when we were actually in a relationship. Instead, I take a deep breath and count to five before replying, "Now's not the time to go into that, Mark. Besides, I didn't think there was anything wrong with our getting together as friends. Just because we had dinner tonight doesn't mean I was hinting at anything else. I'm sorry you took it that way."

"Not sorrier than I am." He sighs, letting my hands drop. "And here I was, thinking we'd be going to your place after this."

And now I remember another reason why we never worked: he's a petulant, manipulative little baby. "You're not interested in the house, I take it," I comment as I lead him to the door.

"Oh, it's gorgeous, but I'd love to give it a little thought."

Right. I know what that means. For every sale, there are at least one or two dozen looky-loos who aren't really interested, but don't know how to tell you so without feeling like a jerk.

"Great," I lie with a smile. "You know my number."

"Yeah, I know your number," he mumbles, as we head towards our car.

# ZACK

I t must smell like the rottenest of rotten eggs in there. Maybe not my finest moment, setting off those stink bombs in the house, but as I sit in my concealed position in the pool house and watch the chaos going on inside, I remind myself there's far too much riding on this for a little thing like ethics to get in the way. Even dick moves are fair in love and war.

My palms get slick as I consider the alternative to not making the sale. My entire career is riding on this. I don't need the money. Just the damn sale. If only she'd accepted my offer, none of this would've been necessary.

Maybe I should tell her the truth, just lay it on the line. She's a reasonable person when she's not acting like a frigid nun. There were brief glimmers of humanity the other night while we were enjoying dinner. At least, I was enjoying it, and it seemed as though she might have been too. She dropped her guard, anyway, and even favored me with a few genuine smiles.

Much more than I ever got before then. It was a start.

Then she turned, became cold and haughty. For no reason at all, her walls were suddenly up. Nah, I can't trust her with the truth. No way. I won't put myself at her mercy. Not when it is extremely unlikely, she'll break down and give me what I need, anyway. No, I'll just have to get the sale fair and square, on my own merits.

Which in this moment just happen to include stink bombs. Because I've evidently regressed to the point where this is a viable option.

But hey, it's working. I watch light after light come on as she runs from room to room. The entire house is lit up before long, blazing like a star in the night. And still she hasn't been able to find the source. I almost feel sorry for her. I'm sure this was the last thing on her mind when she decided to show the property behind my back.

Then, I see the guy who drove up behind her. He stands at one of the windows, opening it to let fresh air in, and I dislike him immediately. He's got one of those square chins that just begs for a fist to smash into it. I've known guys like him my entire life. They're all the same. Pampered, entitled hypocrites.

So what is she doing with him?

She wants the sale.

If there's one thing I can take for granted with Sienna, it's that there's nothing more than a professional relationship here. She probably doesn't even have anything below the waist. Molded plastic, like a doll. Sex doesn't help one's sales figures, which are all that matter to her.

I wish I'd brought binoculars. I can't quite make out what's happening inside. Then again, I hadn't exactly planned on getting a close look. Just knowing that I was ruining her private showing was enough. So I thought.

That was before I got a look at her potential buyer.

I sneak out of the pool house while neither of them is near a window and dash across the back patio, nearly doubled over. Who am I? Some second-rate burglar? Or a Hardy boy? Sneaking around in the dark, peering into windows to get a better look at what's going on inside? Anyone who knows me would laugh at the sight.

What in the ever-loving fuck am I doing still dashing about in the dark. I did what I intended and there's no way a serious showing can go on now, not after Sienna sprinted around the house like she did. With all that square footage, she's got to be exhausted and out of breath. Most definitely unprofessional, which I get the feeling is what she hates most.

But it isn't enough.

For some weird reason I can't walk away. Maybe if the client were anybody else but him. I don't know him, I've never seen him before in my life. But I know his type all too well and I don't like him. I don't like him being in there with her. I don't like the way he looked at her when her back was turned and she was hunting around, looking behind furniture, poking her head into bathrooms. I don't like the way his eyes rake over her body.

The prick!

Even as distaste-bordering-on-rage bubbles up in my chest, I can't help remembering all the times I've checked her out as she walked in front of me. But that's different. I don't know how, specifically, but it just is. I'm not that perv. I didn't practically lick my chops when she bent over. Well, okay, I did, but it was just different.

There's something about the way he looks at her. He moves closer to her. There is something intimate about their pose. I frown in the darkness. Are they more than professional acquaintances? No, they can't be.

*Why not? She's young, gorgeous, and as much as I'd like to believe, more than likely, isn't made of molded plastic down there.* Yes, but this guy? Doesn't she have any taste? I gave her credit for at least that much.

She's closing the windows now and pulling the blinds closed, which means there's less and less I can make out. The lights are going out one by one, too, so the stench has eased, and she's relaxing a little. Damn it. I hoped he would run out, gagging, and drive away.

He must really like the place.

Or...her.

My mood darkens further than ever. Is that it? He's not interested in the house, but her. Shit. My palms are sweaty again.

She takes him back to the entryway, which I can see clearly down the length of the hall which runs from the front to the back of the house. She's laughing good-naturedly, definitely trying to hide her embarrassment. I can see that she is exhausted too. Can't have been easy running around in that tight A-line skirt and those high heels. I can't help but note another stab of guilt in my chest at this.

That's before he…

Reaches for her. Hell, he's placing his hands on her waist. Now he's pulling her a little closer. As if that isn't enough, he's moving in even closer and looking down at her the way a man looks down at the woman he intends to bed.

The bastard.

I don't know if I can stand here and keep watching or if I should just follow what my body is begging me to do. Storm in, fists flying. I can just imagine knocking him on his ass after connecting with that obnoxiously square chin of his. My hands tighten, my heart races. He has no fucking business putting his hands on her.

Wait. What's wrong with me?

I shake my head in an effort to calm myself down and kick those thoughts free. What the hell is wrong with me? First of all, she's *not* my girl. And something tells me she wouldn't appreciate me barging in like some cliché caveman, beating the hell out of a guy just because I don't like his looks or the way he has been eying her up.

Besides, she's catching his hands and very firmly taking them off her waist. The breath I was holding escapes in a rush. She's got things under control. I should've known she would.

"Sorry, asswipe. This one's not for you. Keep moving," I mutter as she lets him down easy. He doesn't deserve that much, but she's graceful enough to preserve his ego.

It's too obvious that he's disappointed. He looks like he

wants to stomp his feet and threaten to hold his breath until he gets what he wants. What did he expect? That they would christen every room of the house together?

His face is wooden as she leads him outside. She locks up behind them.

I wait until the roar of both engines fades into silence before going for my own car, parked at the edge of the property. I chuckle to myself when I remember how she turned him down. I wish I could've heard the exact words she used. Ha, ha, the way his face crumbled when he realized he wasn't getting any tonight.

Serves him right. She should've kneed him in the balls. I've been kneed in the balls before. Twenty years later and I can tell you it's nothing to take lightly. And I wouldn't normally wish it on anyone, but he's a special case. He could use a shift in perspective.

What bothers me more than wishing for another man to experience that sort of pain is the fact that I care so much in the first place. So what if he got a little handsy? She set him straight. Maybe they have a history. I don't know her life.

It just irks the hell out of me to think of another guy touching her that way, thinking he can get away with that sort of thing just because she wants a sale from him. I have no respect for people who think that way, male or female.

Yes, that has to be it.

I slide behind the wheel of the car and pull away from the property. I only detest that bastard because he thought he could take advantage. Not because he was trying to take advantage of Sienna, specifically. I couldn't care less about her. Why would I? She's just my partner in this sale. And she won't even be that if I have my way. Besides, she's got a decent head on her shoulders and she clearly saw right through him.

But as I hit the road, I can't get the image of him with his hands on her out of my head.

"Get a grip, Zack," I growl. The last thing I need in all of this is to let testosterone get in the way of what needs to be done. There's too much riding on this. All that matters is the sale. She can have every sale after this, large or small, I don't care. I just need this one.

Which means it doesn't matter who gets handsy with her. It's none of my business.

Even if that asshole deserved to get punched.

# SIENNA

I don't expect to hear from Mark again, as I steer my way down the circular turnabout and down the wide driveway which leads to the road. He's behind me somewhere. In the past. Just like he was before I called him this afternoon.

But I can still hear the echo of his words in my head. Accusations, more like. I only ever cared about work. I never cared about what he wanted. Is that true?

Not entirely. I cared very much about him. We just didn't have the same priorities, was all. I'm not entirely sure what I need when it comes to a relationship, but I know what I don't need… a man who doesn't get me.

He never did, he never tried. He wanted my body, my adoration, but not me. Not my ambition or my intelligence. He didn't want to hear about my successes. I had nobody to share them with, and he was the only person I wanted to tell when something great happened. Sure, I would call my parents and Tami and they would be excited, but it wasn't the same.

No, he would complain that I was talking about work again. A little part of me understood that he was jealous of my work.

I can't believe I let him get under my skin the way I have again. He doesn't deserve to be there. It's funny how a person can forget, or at least gloss over the truth of the past. If I had remembered more clearly the way things really ended, the real problem between us, I wouldn't have called him at all. No commission is worth it.

I'd been too busy focusing on the sale. Tunnel vision blinded me. That and the need to beat Zack.

My hands tighten around the wheel when I think of him. As if I needed something else to upset me. What would he think if he saw how terribly that 'showing' went? He'd laugh himself sick, no doubt. Even more reason why it's good that he never knows about it.

Men. What a pain in general. No wonder I've been single for so long. I haven't missed the drama, for sure. And I haven't missed feeling like there's something wrong with me for being ambitious and liking what I do for a living. For wanting to be good at it. Not just good, but the best.

It's a relief to get home, to be alone. Nobody wants anything from me here. I can slide out of my heels and into a pair of slippers before going up to my room. Sometimes I wonder if a studio apartment would make more sense for me than a full house, since I rarely spend time in anything but the kitchen and the bedroom. But I do like the thought of owning space, even if I don't take advantage of it.

What would it have been like if I'd allowed Mark to follow me here? We'd be going upstairs together. I wouldn't have to be alone. But that's no reason to be with somebody, just to keep from being alone. I haven't sunk that far yet.

And I have no intention of ever doing so.

As I wash my face, I think about any other contacts I can reach out to. There's bound to be somebody interested on the list of people I've been working on for years now. I'm pretty sure I'd miss my contact list more than I'd miss my arm if I ever lost it.

By the time I'm back in my room, with an old movie on the TV and the laptop open beside me, I'm ready to send a few emails. One of them will be to Mark, to follow-up on our showing and to thank him for dinner. He might be a manipulative, sulky baby, but he knows plenty of people through his father's law firm and they know lots of wealthy people, too. It's never a good idea to burn bridges.

What would it be like to tell him what I really think about him? Maybe not quite as satisfying as it would be to tell Zack off, but close enough.

There's Zack again!

I can't seem to keep him out of my thoughts for very long. I tell myself not to stress about it. It's to be expected: we're working together. I won't be rid of him until the house is sold. After that, he's toast in my head, but not before I tell him off but good for trying to screw me over today.

It's thoughts of that event that keep me working long into the night.

It is nearly two in the morning when I stop and stretch. A

feeling of slow languor hits my body. I've worked hard, I deserve a break. I head for the bathroom, run a bath, and strip. Naked, I pour fragrant oil in the steaming water. Then I light a strawberry scented candle. Slipping one foot into the silky water, I sigh with luscious pleasure.

To hell with Zack. And his strong, masculine hands. And his hard jaw. And that flat stomach.

The sensation of the hot bubbles enveloping my body is tantalizing. The candle provides an extra touch of sensuality as it pulsates its sultry light across the curves of my body. I run my hands down the silky smoothness of my shape. My nipples are firm and erect.

Yes, I'm aroused, but it's not Zack.

Not at all. It's just that I haven't had a man or climaxed for such a long time. There is a new and mysterious fire inside me that needs quenching. I imagine myself lying on my bed, naked but for my four-inch high red stilettos. There are pillows under my hips, and I'm slowly spreading open my legs for the man standing at the bottom of the bed. After-noon sun beams in illuminating my spread open body for him. I try to imagine that he is Mark or some faceless stranger, but he morphs into Zack.

Fine, whatever. It's just a fantasy. It doesn't mean anything. People fantasize about taking part in orgies, it doesn't mean they actually want to do it in real life. As much as I want to be angry with myself for not being firmer with myself, I can't deny that I'm curious where this is going to go.

*"Spread your legs wider so I can see your wet pussy," Zack orders. He strokes his erection through his trousers.*

*Once, when he was sitting opposite me at dinner - my gaze accidentally dropped down and I saw his bulge it...was big. Very big. I widen my legs in the most provocative and sexy way I can as I feel my pussy open up to receive him.*

*"I always knew you were talented," he says throatily.*

A wave of heat bursts through me, and my imagination starts running wild and vivid. *I see him undo his belt. "Mmmm." His hard dick stands proud. Thick, angry looking veins snake around it. It wants to enter me. I am ready for him.* My hand moves to caress my clit. "Oh, yes." A wave of pleasure runs through my body. Completely immersed in my fantasy, I watch him come closer. *His large hands cup my breasts. They are full and heavy with excitement. He bends his dark head and licks one nipple while pinching the other in his fingers.* A gasp slips out of my mouth and my body aches. The feeling is almost more than I can bear.

*"I can't wait anymore. I've got to taste you," he mutters thickly, as his powerful hands curve under my butt and lifts my hips up to his mouth. His tongue pushes  deep into me, hot, velvety, and insatiable.*

My spine arches as I stroke around the hood of my clit ever so softly. I want to make this last, but I can feel the waves of pleasure getting stronger. *Starting from where his mouth works hungrily to the tips of my fingers and toes.* Oh, but it is glorious. When my fingers accidentally brush against my clit, I jump at the intense sensation. Despite it all, there's an empty sensation inside me.

*Zack lifts his head and looks at me, his beautiful eyes, dark with passion.*

*Tingles dance across my skin. "I can't last much longer. Get inside me," I whisper.*

*He stands, grabs my ankles in his hands, and pushes them all the way forward until my body is almost folded in half as my pussy and ass are both completely exposed to him. The look in his eyes is electric. With a dark chuckle, he presses the tip of his thick cock at my slit and looking into my eyes, pushes down.*

I plunge my fingers into my pussy as deep as they will go and thrust them in and out of myself faster and faster following the rhythm set by the image of Zack's dick slamming into me. Slower, faster, it all feels fantastic.

*"I'm going to come inside you," he roars.*

That's enough to send me over the edge. An intense orgasm grips me hard and shakes me, the reverberations making my body convulse. Water sloshes out of the tub and my head flips back and smashes the taps behind me.

"Owww," I groan, rubbing the back of my head, and coming down with a bump in the foggy bathroom. That'll teach me not to fantasize about that creep again. Still, it was a really powerful orgasm.

## SIENNA

"Well, well, well," I whisper, leaning in to get a closer look at the stats on the listing. There have been over two hundred and fifty hits on that specific page since it went live yesterday afternoon. Less than twenty-four hours ago. Not bad.

Twenty-three of those visitors dropped a line via the site's comment form. Another good sign. I've been around long enough to know that most visitors who click on a listing such as this one are just looking around for fun. Fantasizing about what they'd do with a house like that. Printing out the photos for their vision boards, I don't know.

For nearly ten percent of my visitors to ask for more information is good news.

I just might pat myself on the back.

But not yet. Not until I have a signature…in ink.

Now's the time to start wading through the messages, figuring out which ones look to have potential and which ones clearly don't. I find that the people who take the time to ask pointed questions, such as exactly when they might be able to come in and look at the house, are the ones who are the most serious. They want a time, they want a date, they're busy and they respect that I'm busy, too. I like those people.

The knock at my door is nothing but background noise. "Yes?" I murmur, only half paying attention.

"Good morning, partner."

Oh. Him. I guess it was too much for me to hope he had mysteriously disappeared off the face of the Earth overnight. It's a good thing my face is turned to the monitor, or else he'd see the unpleasant red my face has become.

I take a deep breath and wipe my expression of all reaction before turning to him, blocking the view of what I'm working on. "Good morning. What can I do for you?"

He blinks, a little startled. It's a minor victory I can't help silently rejoicing over. Otherwise, he's the picture of calm composure, the way he always tries to look. I've seen him shaken already. I know it's possible.

And it's way too much fun to watch his mask slip a little. I can't help it.

"What do you think you can do for me?" he asked, sliding right back into his slimy act.

I'm starting to wonder if it's an act at all. Maybe this is just who he is. I hope not, for his sake. I manage to hold my temper back, but just barely. "You're the one who came in here and disturbed me. You're the one who obviously wants something. What is it? I'm very busy."

"Yes, I'm sure you are." Rather than getting down to business, he leans against the waist-high filing cabinet that sits along the far wall. His biceps bulge and strain against his sleeves when he folds his arms.

It's an effort to pry my eyes from them. And it's a bigger effort to not let them slide down to the bulge in his pants. "So?" I lean back in my chair, crossing my legs. Two can play at this game—if this is a game at all. I'm still not sure. Maybe it's just my hormones out of control. I've always been able to control them in the past, but he's a different beast. It must be the way he already manages to aggravate me. My blood is already simmering after just a few moments of exposure.

He clears his throat. I'm making him uncomfortable. What a shame. "I was wondering how the listing is doing."

"You could've checked that out for yourself."

"Only one person can be signed into the page at a time and you know it," he says, his icy eyes narrowing. "I can't check the stats if you plan on hogging them all day."

"I would hardly call performing due diligence hogging the stats," I mutter, my head tilted to the side. "I'm working on a list of interested parties based on requests for information. How is that hogging?"

"You know what I mean. Get your information and sign out, so somebody else can sign in. Or," he continues, tilting his head to mock me, "tell me what you're working on and we can work on it together. After all, we're supposed to be doing this as a team."

My blood goes from simmering to a rolling boil. "Oh, now you want to be a team?" I ask, fighting to keep my voice under control, if not my blood pressure. "After what you've done to me so far? You flat-out told me to give you the listing. Then, you tried to bogart the entire meeting with Nick by deliberately scheduling it at a completely different time of day than you originally offered. And I'm the one who has a problem being a team player? How do you keep from laughing out loud at some of the things you say?"

"Don't pretend to be so innocent." He chuckles humorlessly. "You have a few tricks up your sleeve."

"What's that supposed to mean?"

"Just what I said." He shrugs. "And I don't hold it against you. Really, I don't. You don't get to be as good as you are, or as I am, without knowing your way around the rules. If anything, I'm thankful to finally have a formidable opponent."

"I'm not supposed to be your opponent," I remind him through clenched teeth. "We're supposed to be working together."

"Which is why you're single-handedly managing the listing? Which is why I had no say in the wording? And now I can't get into the backend to analyze the traffic to the page?"

"You're the one who set the tone for this entire undertaking. If you'd just gone along with me from the get-go, during dinner, all of this would have gone much differently."

"That again."

"Yes, that again!"

A few laughs float our way over the cubicle walls, and I realize I was shouting. My cheeks burn as I duck my head, clearing my throat. The back of my neck feels all prickly and hot, and the top of my head is about to blow clear off. I take a few deep breaths.

"Feel better?" he murmurs.

My head snaps up, my eyes burning a hole into his. "Yes. I feel much better. Thanks." I leave out the part where my hands are practically twitching, wanting to strangle him.

He arches one eyebrow. "Good. Honestly, if I didn't know better, I would think you had a bad night last night. Maybe a date didn't go as planned. Or something like that." He walks out, closing the door behind him, before I have the chance to come up with a retort.

What is there to say? My mouth hangs open as my brain struggles to catch up.

What was that supposed to mean?

He can't know about the showing. Can he? No, impossible. Unless he's been stalking me. Maybe stalking is too serious a word. Even though I wouldn't put it past him.

Is that it? Did he follow me to the house? If so, why didn't he announce his presence?

No, no, I'm being paranoid. I'm also biting my nails, which is a habit I thought I broke myself of a long time ago. But I'm nervous. I'm rarely nervous like this.

Well, what's the worst that could happen even if he were to find out that I was going behind his back? Nothing, that's what. I need to get back some of the confidence I had last night, when I was telling myself he was getting no less than he deserved for stabbing me in the back. He started this.

It's one thing to be confident when I'm home, in my pajamas.

It's another when I'm face-to-face with him and he's staring at me with those ridiculous eyes of his and I don't know whether I want him to keep staring into their crazy-beautiful depths, or swallow glass and die from it.

I just don't know.

There's one thing I'm still certain of—I need to sell this damn house.

And fast.

## ZACK

Zack

R ight. She lied with a straight face!

A reluctant smile plays at the corner of my lips. I started the ball rolling, but good to know she's more than willing to play dirty. Good, because I can now stop feeling guilty. All is fair in love and war.

I stroll over to the coffee room. The coffee is shit, but it's a den of absolutely invaluable up-to-date information. Mary Ann Colter bounces up to me. Behind her glasses her eyes are shining. I like her. Not my type, but she has that librarian appeal. I have a feeling she would be a live wire in bed.

"It's my birthday on Friday and I'm having a party at my place on Saturday. Wanna come?"

I hesitate. A birthday party full of people I don't know doesn't sound too appealing.

"I have a friend I'd like to introduce you to. She's really nice and gorgeous too."

Now, I know I definitely don't want to go. "Thanks for the invite, but this weekend is kinda busy with this sale and all."

"Oh! Never mind, maybe next time?"

"Next time," I echo with a smile.

"Right. I'll text you my address in case you change your mind," she calls as she skips away.

Brad sidles up to me. "How it going with QB?"

Oh, did I mention that is Sienna's nickname around the office. It stands for Queen Bitch.

I grin. "Not bad. She's actually quite fun."

"No kidding?"

I laugh at his shocked expression, then shake my head. "Nope."

He frowns. "So should I put money on the bet?"

"No, don't do that," I say hastily, looking around me.

The guys have a cringe-worthy bet going that I'll end up in bed with Sienna. No amount of persuasion will get them to drop it. Last time I looked the total was already nearly three hundred dollars.

Hell, if Sienna finds out about the bet, she'll throw a fit like the office has never seen.

# SIENNA

Two-thirty.

Where is he?

I've been waiting to hear from him again. Actually, I've been waiting all day, as much as I'd rather not admit to myself that I have been. I'm not exactly proud of who Zack has reduced me to. We're like two kids fighting on the playground. I'm surprised we haven't devolved to kicking and hair pulling.

Then again, it's only been two days. We still have time for things to go further down the tubes.

I'm so desperate to find him without making it look like I'm looking for him that I even go to the break room and make a cup of coffee. I hardly ever do this, as the coffee here is swill, the sort that comes out of those pod machines. I have to be frugal to pay off my large mortgage, but I'm willing to shell out a little extra dough for decent coffee.

He's not one of the smattering of people gathered around, chatting. He isn't parading himself through the office like he's God's gift to women, which is unusual for him. He's not even kissing Rodney's ass in his office. And the few times I've casually strolled past his cubicle, it's been empty.

Where is the jerk?

"Forget this," I mutter, tossing the crappy coffee down the drain and marching out of the break room. So what if everybody who witnessed me doing that whispers to each other, wondering why I'm acting crazy? They probably already think I'm nuts.

I have a feeling. A very bad feeling.

He's pulling his next move. Right now, this very minute. He's doing something sneaky and thinks he's going to get away with it. "We'll see about that," I whisper to myself, teeth clenched as I punch my arms into the sleeves of my coat and grab my purse.

Minutes later, I'm on the road, driving to the house. What's the worst that could happen? I could show up and find it empty, just like I left it last night. No big deal. I'll simply go back to the office and play nice.

But I didn't get as far as I've come in this business by ignoring my instincts. They're screaming at me as I drive down the freeway, grateful for the almost nonexistent traffic at this time of day. I need to get to the house, fast, before he has the chance to do anything I can't undo.

It's a beautiful, sunny day, if slightly chilly, and the mid-afternoon sun glints off the chrome of Zack's sports car as I pull into the roundabout. "I knew it! I knew it!" I shout, squeezing the steering wheel the way I'd love to squeeze his neck.

Or maybe a certain part of his body he'd regret having squeezed much more.

There's a car parked beside his. Not as flashy as Zack's, but very expensive and foreign. The kind of person who could afford a pile like this. After taking a quick glance at myself in the rearview mirror and forcing my face into more pleasant lines - nobody ever sold a house by charging in, looking like an escapee from the loony bin - I step out of my car and stride confidently up to the front door.

"Hello?" I call out, my tone light and pleasant.

A pair of footsteps echo off the marble floors as Zack and another man come in from the library. I've often heard of a person looking like they were caught with their pants down, but I've never quite seen the expression on a person's face until just now. He literally looks as though I caught him doing something dirty.

Because I did.

"I thought you were busy this afternoon," he says, immediately putting on an act for the client's sake. Charming, good-natured, a real team player.

It's enough to make me want to throw up all over the marble beneath my feet.

"My appointment had to be rescheduled," I inform him, flashing a brilliant smile to rival his. "And I knew you'd want me to meet this gentleman. Hello. I'm Sienna, Zack's partner." I walk to him with my head high and my hand extended, still smiling.

He smiles in return, his eyes flitting over me in a quick, practiced maneuver before locking onto mine. He's skilled in the art of appreciating women, I can tell. And although he's a bit old for me, maybe in his late forties, I wouldn't kick him out of bed for eating crackers. Thick, gorgeous salt-and-pepper hair, brilliant green eyes, a warm smile and a suit that looks as though it was made with him in mind.

This will be easy.

Zack clears his throat. "Sienna, this is Kent Holloway. I'm glad the two of you are getting the chance to meet up."

*Oh, I'll just bet you are. I'll just bet you're over the moon with excitement.* "So am I," I murmur, never taking my eyes from Kent's. As far as I'm concerned, there's only one man in the room. In the entire world, for that matter.

At least, that's what I'll let him think.

I can't help but notice an absolutely mouthwatering aroma in the air. "Mm, what's that wonderful smell?" I ask, looking from Kent to Zack. Is it my imagination, or is Zack blushing just a little bit? No, it can't be. Men like him don't blush.

"Oh, some places just smell good. You know how it is." Zack chuckles.

I turn to Kent. "I don't suppose you're wearing cologne that smells just like freshly baked apple pie, do you?"

"Not lately." He grins. "Though, I could be convinced, if that's the sort of thing a lady like you enjoys."

"Oh, you!" I laugh, tossing my hair over one shoulder. It really is too easy sometimes. "I suppose it's better on the old waistline than an actual slice of pie, though. Well. You look like a busy man. Let's get down to business, then, shall we?"

"By all means. I enjoy a lady who knows how to take charge of a situation."

We share another laugh—really, the things a woman has to put up with sometimes—and then we get started. "I don't know about you, but I do love this entry," I muse, looking up. "The spaciousness of it. The light the window above the front door allows in, reflecting off the chandelier."

"Beautiful," he agrees.

I don't think he's looking at the chandelier when he says it, but I pretend not to notice. "I don't know if you had time to check out the library yet...?" I deliberately avoid Zack's pointed stare as I lead the way.

"We didn't have much time to explore," Kent explains. "Besides, I would love to get a woman's viewpoint on it."

"Oh?"

He nods, shrugging. "I find that women have a little more imagination when it comes to what a home can become."

"You know, that is so true," I concede, nodding slowly as I pretend to think this over. "We have the vision. At least, that's what I've always heard."

"And who have you heard that from?" Zack asks, standing behind Kent, so I'm the only one who can see the look of utter fury on his face.

"Plenty of people." I shrug, pretending not to notice or care that his head is close to exploding. "Anyway, here you can see what the previous owner used as a library-slash-music room, but it has potential to be used as a study, a family room, whatever the owner's heart desires."

We go to the kitchen from there. "I would kill for the chance to own a stove like this one. I believe it was flown in from England," I say when we walk in. "Six burners, plus a built-in grill, beside a dual oven. What I couldn't do with that."

"You enjoy cooking?" Kent asks, amused.

"I love it. I wish I had more time to do it. Work." I shrug. "You know how it is."

He chuckles. "Yes, I know very well. But if I didn't work as hard as I do, I wouldn't be in the market for a home like this, would I?"

"It would appear as though you and I think along the same lines, Mr. Holloway."

We share another warm smile as Zack fumes silently.

This is rapidly turning into one of my favorite showings of all time. Maybe one of my favorite days ever—full stop.

"What do you think about the bathrooms?" Kent asks as we walk along the second-floor hallway. "Would you consider the master bath worthy of a sophisticated, worldly woman such as yourself?"

"Is it lavish enough, do you mean?" I grin.

"Precisely."

"I believe so." We step in together, Zack trailing behind. "I mean, the walk-in tub with sixteen jets? That alone would be reason to spend half my life in this room. Then, you have the massive shower, a steam room, heated floors. It's like a trip to the spa without ever having to leave the comfort of home. Combine that with an adjacent walk-in closet bigger than my current bedroom and I'm in heaven."

He laughs, the rich sound echoing off the floor and walls. "You sound like an easy woman to please."

"Oh, I wouldn't go that far." I smirk, shaking my head. "I'm also a fan of the ten years still left on the roof's warrantee, the brand-new dual zone HVAC system, and the energy efficient windows. Without those things, the cost of keeping a home this size comfortable would be unimaginable. I'm a very practical woman, too."

"So I see," he murmurs. "I've been so busy admiring all this beauty, I forgot to ask the really tough questions. I thank you for anticipating my interest."

"That's my job, after all."

We all but link arms as we leave the master suite, exploring the other bedrooms and discussing trivialities. If he wants the house, he knows it by now. I don't think he does, but playing nice like this is clearly ruining Zack's day.

That makes the charade so worthwhile.

"Are you a sailing man, Mr. Holloway?" I ask as we step outside, where amber rays of sun sparkle on the lake. The gentle lapping of waves against the shore is hypnotic, utterly relaxing.

"I've been known to sail on occasion, but I would much rather just sit out here and take in the view. Are there fish in the lake?"

"Oh, yes," Zack interjects. "Great fishing out here."

Kent blinks in surprise before letting out that booming laugh of his. "Good lord! I almost forgot you were with us!" He laughs again.

I join in while staring straight at my so-called partner. "I'm sure you could be forgiven, with all of this to take in at once." I spread my arms wide, indicating the lake and the property behind us. "I don't think I'd ever go to the office again, if I had a home like this."

"By all means, let's arrange for you to get one right away." Zack smiles at me.

"What would you do without me?" I tease, shooting daggers his way when Kent isn't looking.

"I'm sure the sight of you walking into the office every morning is a real treat for all those who have the pleasure of working with you," Kent observes, his eyes warm and familiar as he smiles down at me.

"Hmm. I think Zack might beg to differ. We haven't always worked together. I'm afraid I've given him a run for his money on more than one property. Isn't that right?" I walk off before he has the chance to answer, back up to the house.

Kent follows at my heels, the way I'd expect him to, while Zack brings up the rear.

Just the way it should be.

## SIENNA

Two days pass without much friction between the two of us. I'm pretty sure he's learned his lesson now.

I'm sure it helps that I was the bigger person on the whole Kent Holloway thing. I didn't call Zack out on his shenanigans when Kent drove away, and he didn't give me any grief about it. Even I can admit he's smart enough not to need things spelled out for him.

He messes with the bull, he gets the horns. It's as simple as that.

Of course, Kent called me later that evening to see if I'd be interested in going to dinner with him. I told him I appreciated the offer and was flattered, but didn't think it would be right. "After all, how would it look if anyone else discovered I went to dinner with a potential buyer?" I asked.

"I don't need to be a potential buyer, if that's what's standing in your way," he offered.

He had the nerve to act surprised when I wasn't bowled over

by his chivalry. I guess I should have expected it. The way I was flirting with him. I would never have done that if I had been so desperate to annoy Zack and ruin his showing. On the bright side, the Kent situation did serve a purpose.

Zack knows for sure who he's dealing with. I think it might even have humbled him a little, since I haven't had the dubious honor of dealing with him since then. To be fair, he hasn't been sneaking around, either. He's always in the office, either on a call or furiously pounding out messages on his laptop.

I know, because I've been making the rounds. I've fixed and choked down more cups of hideous coffee than I care to remember, all in the spirit of giving me an excuse to walk past his cubicle.

Just after such an excursion, while sitting back down at my desk, I see that I have a new message. The subject: Open House.

*Any thoughts on the open house?*

I roll my eyes and fight the urge to stand on my chair and yell at him across the field of cubicles between us. I just walked by, for heaven's sake. He saw me. I know he did. But he chose to be passive aggressive and send an email, instead.

Wimp. Taking the easy way out and avoiding face-to-face confrontation.

Wait. What am I so irritated over? I prefer it this way. Not having to look at his smug smile. It's like he's giving me a present.

I look back over his extremely articulate and well-thought-out email before firing off a quick reply: *Lots and lots.*

I can't help giggling a little as I send it, wondering what his reaction will be. For the first time, I wish we sat closer than we do. I would like to hear the sounds he makes.

Almost instantly, he sends a reply of his own.

*Care to share with the rest of the team?*

"No, I damn well wouldn't," I whisper, growling a little in the back of my throat. My fingers fly over the keys.

*What about you? I don't like the feeling that I'm the lab partner who does all the work while the other one only pretends.*

This time, I hear his response loud and clear. "Only pretends?" It carries across the room, laced with more than a little rancor.

Before he has the chance to send anything, I add,

*It's just an example. If it cuts a little too close, maybe you're feeling guilty?*

I'm rewarded with the sound of sputtering from the other side of the office, which leaves me leaning back in my chair with a satisfied smile. Getting under his skin is almost better than sex.

Not that I've had the real thing any time recently to make a fair comparison.

He has a point, of course. He generally does. He just stinks at getting it across. The open house is in two days and it's got to be spectacular. I have a list of the vendors I normally use for events of a higher magnitude, but I've never sold a house like this before. Still, they should do just fine.

But what about him? What does he like to do for events such as this? He is right. I have to talk to him about it and without starting a fight, without name calling, or flinging thinly-veiled insults at each other. I hate to admit that he might have a better game plan in place than me, but the most important concern is landing the sale.

My pride might have to be put on the back burner for now.

I step out of my cubicle with every intention of going to him and suggesting a truce when I slam into a brick wall, instead. A brick wall dressed in a thin-striped blue and white shirt and matching blue tie.

The tie matches his eyes, I realize on looking up into them. Son of a bitch. He even matched his tie to his eyes.

Those eyes narrow as he stares down at me. "Here." He steps back and thrusts toward me a now-crumpled piece of paper, thanks to our collision.

My body tingles. "What's this?"

"A list of the vendors I had in mind for the open house. What do you think? A *lab report?*" He sneers, not bothering to hide the fact that my off-handed remark got to him.

I wasn't even trying, for Pete's sake.

"Oh. Thank you. I was about to come over and talk to you—"

"Yeah, well, there's no need for that now. Is there?"

"I guess not. But don't you think—"

"Don't I think what?" he demands with a sigh.

I look down at the list, my cheeks burning more than just a little. I wish he didn't make me blush like this. Why am I blushing in the first place? That's a better question, come to think of it. "Don't you think we should decide who to use, between your list and mine? I mean, I have a list of my own."

"I had expected as much," he replies with all the patience of a man who has something else he'd much rather be doing right now. "But since you seem to know so much about the house and you have the *vision* and everything, I thought you would want to be the one to deal with this."

"Now, wait just a minute," I warn, drawing myself up to my full height in preparation for a fight. Why does it always have to come to this with us?

"No, you wait a minute. You've been at the controls all along, so why would you have a problem with remaining there now?"

"Because… because I thought we might, in fact, work better as a team. I'm not the one scheduling secret showings behind the other one's back."

"Oh, aren't you?" he asks, eyebrows shooting up. "You might want to have a talk with yourself about truth and your idea of it before you go around slinging bald-faced lies like that one."

"And what do you mean by that?"

"I mean just what I said," he sneers. "Save the innocent act for someone who'll buy it, because I don't. You're insulting me and degrading yourself."

The paper crumples even further in my hand as it clenches in a tight fist. "How dare you?" I hiss. "You're lucky we're in the office right now and not out in the street somewhere, because I'd tell you just exactly what I think of you."

"Why don't you just send it in an email?" he asks smugly, knowing he got the last word as he turns and saunters away.

I'm too furious to move. Blood rushes in my ears. My knees are weak. There's a tightness in my chest. I want to scream.

Yes, and get fired. No matter how great my sales record is, nobody wants to work with someone who loses control, screams, and causes a ruckus.

I settle for going back to my desk, closing the door, and opening my mouth in a silent scream. That doesn't do much to assuage my fury.

God, who does he think he is?

## SIENNA

T he knock at the door rips me out of my scream and makes me freeze. "Who is it?"

"Becca." She opens the door a crack and peeks in. "You don't usually ask who's knocking. Is everything all right?"

"Of course." I take a deep, shuddery breath before sitting down. "Sorry. I was just a little worked up at that exact moment. I'm fine now. I didn't mean to be rude." My legs are still shaking with unspent rage.

"But you're okay?" She doesn't look convinced.

"I'm definitely okay." I smile to prove my point. "What's up?"

"I was just stopping by to see how things were going between you and Mr. Gorgeous." She bats her eyelashes, fanning herself.

My smile slips a notch. "Oh. Him."

"Yeah, him." She giggles. "I saw the two of you talking just now. I swear, I was waiting for one of you to jump the other's bones."

That's the last thing I expected to hear and definitely, the last thing I was in the mood to do when he was in front of me. I scowl at her. "You are deeply disturbed, Becca."

"You mean to tell me you don't feel it? I mean, Jesus. The temperature jumped past the boiling point, and you weren't even touching each other."

"Did you hear what we were saying?" I venture.

"No. Unfortunately, I could only see your mouths moving from over at my desk," she admits, "but the passion was clearly there."

"Passion? You've been reading too many books with ripped bodices," I tease. "Things like that don't happen in real life."

"What things?"

"You know. The two of us having such a passionate conversation that we suddenly start tearing at each other's clothes. It doesn't happen. Especially not between the two of us."

"You're sure about that?"

"I don't think I've ever been so sure about anything in my life. If you're looking to play matchmaker, or expecting to walk in on the two of us banging it out in the supply closet, you're sadly mistaken."

"Boo." She leans against the filing cabinet, arms crossed.

The gesture reminds me of what Zack did, just a couple of days ago. I wish I could stop thinking about him at random times. "Sorry to disappoint you," I singsong, shrugging.

"I'm not the only one who would be disappointed, you know."

For half a second, maybe less, I think she's going to say Zack would be disappointed if nothing were to happen between us. Could that be true? I wouldn't put it past him. He probably thinks I'm dying with love for him and would be annoyed if he found out I couldn't care less about his many charms.

She continues, "Half the office would hate finding out they were wrong about you guys."

Oh, this is much worse than anything I could've come up with on my own. "Wait. What are you saying?"

She leans closer, eyes wide, whispering, "I'm saying, everybody's talking about the two of you working together, that's what. Everybody has seen the sparks flying."

She might as well have poured a bucket of ice water over my head. "Oh, no. That's not true, is it?"

"Why would I lie?"

"I don't know, but I wish you were." To my surprise, I do something I've never done before. The distress is such I wring my hands. This is just about the worst thing that could've happened. Any little bit of credibility I've fought for in this company would be for nothing. I can't have them looking at me as some bubble-headed, hair-brained weakling who can't keep a good head on her shoulders when there's a handsome man in the vicinity.

"Don't take it so seriously," she urges, waving her hands. "It's not as if we're placing bets on the wedding date, for God's sake. You always take everything too seriously."

"My work is serious to me."

"Understood," she whispers, placating me.

I hate that. As if I were a toddler, she's calming.

"No, you don't understand." I wish there was a way to explain the hurricane of emotion roaring in my head, but I can't even explain it to myself. She wouldn't understand how touchy the subject of Zack really is to me.

Even if she's the only person in the company, who's anywhere close to a friend I can't tell her how frustrating it is to work with him. The last thing I need is for Rodney's assistant to know how difficult a time we're having with working together.

"He's really got you worked up, hasn't he?"

I shake my head in the face of her knowing smile. This, right here, is why making work friends is a hassle. "No, not the way you think. He's a challenge, for sure. We're both pretty set in our ways, but it's going well. And not the way you think, either."

"All right, all right." She pouts a little as she straightens up, her hand on the doorknob. "Forgive me for thinking it was fun that the two hottest people in the company are about to give us a bit of interesting gossip. This place is so boring, we all need a little something to brighten our days."

"The two hottest?" I smirk, rolling my eyes. "Doubtful. And I'm sorry to ruin your diversions. I don't mean to."

"Yeah, right. Spoilsport." She sticks her tongue out at me just before leaving.

I repay the compliment as the door closes with a soft click.

Then I bury my head in my arms and wish I were dead.

This can't be happening. How long have they all been whispering? All week, I guess. And they probably notice when I walk past Zack's door, and how many times a day I've been doing it. Plus, they were probably watching while the two of us argued outside my cubicle. Granted, it was quiet enough that it didn't sound like an argument, but I'm not sure if I'd rather they know what it was or not. What's worse, arguing or having a lover's spat?

Either way, it was not very professional of me. Either way, I'm screwed.

Only one person comes to mind. I pick up my phone and dial almost without having to look at the screen. "Tami? I need a drink. Can you meet me tonight?"

"Sure thing!" she bubbles. "There's so much I want to talk over with you too. About the wedding."

Good. It'll give me something to think about other than my misery. "Terrific. I can hardly wait."

So now, it's just a matter of making it through the rest of the day without taking an early Happy Hour. Is it considered poor form to start drinking before noon?

# SIENNA

"To Thirsty Thursdays," my sister announces, raising her glass with a flourish. She's already four margaritas in.

I'm glad she's taking an Uber home as I raise my glass, too. "Sure. Whatever you say." We both laugh, and mine is actually a real laugh, thanks to the three margaritas I've already consumed. Good thing greasy bar food exists to soak up all the alcohol.

I've never quite known if that is scientifically true, but I know it worked for me in college.

"So, did you look at the dress pictures I sent you?" Tami asks before shoving a pile of nachos into her mouth.

We both find it hilarious when she dribbles guacamole down her chin.

"What a slob I am," she announces.

I finish my drink and raise my hand for another.

"Well did you?" Tami prompts, a note of seriousness has crept into her voice.

I nod at the barman, then wave my finger at our empty glasses. He nods back. I turn back to my sister. "Yes, I did."

"What do you think?"

"I think—" A shove from an elbow belonging to a drunk man passing behind my chair interrupts me. He doesn't apologize and I shoot him a dirty look before continuing, "I think they're all pretty."

"But none of them jumped out at you, huh?" A frown creases her brow.

"Does it really matter whether or not they jump out at me?" I ask, tilting my head to the side. "I mean it. Sincerely. This is your wedding. Since when does it matter how the brides-maids feel about their dresses?"

"Ouch."

I place a hand on her arm, squeezing. "I didn't mean that as an insult to you. I think it's amazing that you want to give us input on the dress we'd feel most comfortable in. But all of us have different body types. Laurie's tall and athletic, Kyra's tiny and petite, Mary's plus-size, I've got these bad boys." I point to my sizeable chest before it occurs to me that maybe I shouldn't be referencing my boobs in the middle of a crowded bar.

Tami's face falls. "You're right. What are we going to do? We'll never find one that suits all of you equally. Somebody's going to be unhappy and that's what I'm trying so hard not to let happen."

"Why not just pick the color and let us choose the dress that suits us best? I mean, it seems like the store carries most styles in every color, so we can all feel confident and comfortable in something we've chosen for ourselves."

Just like that, her eyes well up with tears. "This is why you're my Maid of Honor. You know that, right?"

"Funny. I thought that was because I'm the best sister in the entire world. And as best sister and Maid of Honor, I will be eating the last of the nachos."

"Please, I shouldn't be eating them in the first place. You're not the one who has to squeeze into a wedding dress in six months."

"And you'll look just as gorgeous then as you do now," I promise, sweeping the last chip all over the platter to catch every last bit of topping left behind. It isn't often that I let myself indulge like this. I deserve it.

"Gorgeous? Please," she scoffs.

"You think I'm kidding? Meanwhile, the guy who's been checking you out for the last five minutes agrees with me. He's at your nine o'clock," I advise before eating the loaded chip.

Tami looks around casually, the practiced gesture of a pretty girl who's used to getting checked out. She makes sure the diamond ring on her left hand is plainly visible though.

"Oof..." I giggle, turning my head in the other direction. "You crushed him, babe."

"If he has half a brain in his head, he'll turn his attention to you," she declares.

"No, thanks. I don't want your rejects. Besides," I observe after glancing his way. "He's not interested in me. He's back to watching the ball game on the TV behind the bar."

She cranes her neck, looking around the room, as the bartender places fresh drinks in front of us. "There's got to be someone here for you."

I stop just shy of spitting the mouthful of my drink all over her. "Hold on! I never said I was interested in anybody here. Jeez!"

"You're a young woman. You're hot. You're a total boss. You need to get laid more often, I think."

"Wow. This is *so* the conversation I was hoping to have tonight."

"And if you don't start dating somebody soon, you won't be able to ask him to be your date to the wedding. Because that's not the sort of invitation you can just randomly make, you know. It can only be a person you've been dating for long enough to warrant something so important."

"Have you been reading wedding etiquette articles again? Because you sound like you're reading one of them right now."

"Seriously."

"Seriously," I agree, nodding. "I never said I even wanted a date for the wedding. I'm gonna be pretty busy taking care of you that day."

"But who's gonna take care of you?"

I shrug. "I guess I'll have to handle myself, too."

"No, Sienna, that's no good," she slurs, staring into my eyes. "I want you to be happy. And to have lots of orgasms."

"Could you not?" I hiss, my eyes darting around. "I don't need anybody coming up and offering to help, thanks. And you know what? I had the opportunity earlier this week, and I turned it down."

"With who?"

Uh-oh. This is not going to impress her very much. I shouldn't have said anything. "Mark."

Her mouth falls open, eyes wide. "Shut up. If you hadn't turned him down, I'd beat the crap out of you right now in front of all these people. Best sister or not. He's a dick."

I straighten my spine. "He's not a dick. Anyway, I'm just saying, your sister is doing just fine for herself."

Her laughter doesn't do much for my self-esteem. "Um, sorry to disappoint you, but an indecent proposal from your jerk of an ex doesn't exactly ease my mind. Thanks very much."

"I had a prospective client ask me to dinner yesterday. He would've jumped on the Sienna Express."

Her eyes go round, like little saucers. "Tell me you said yes."

I sigh. "I think he's old enough to be our father." She deflates so spectacularly that I almost burst out laughing. "But he keeps it tight," I add helpfully.

Her laughter rings out, a little louder than normal, thanks to the alcohol. "I love *Drunk Sienna*. You're so much more fun than *Sober Sienna*. She would never talk about keeping it tight."

Her words sting more than she knows. I tell myself it's only because the drinks have left me feeling a little more sensitive than usual. There's nothing wrong with her teasing me, and she has a point. Sober Sienna can be a real stick in the mud.

Tami finally notices my expression and the way I'm obviously not having fun anymore, because she stops laughing. "Oh. I'm sorry. I didn't mean I don't like you otherwise. I'm just saying…"

I force a smile. "I'm too serious most of the time. I get it. I do. It's not like I want to be so serious. I'm just always…"

"Thinking about serious things," she finishes.

"Right."

Her eyes light up. "I forgot!"

"What did you forget?"

"You're the one who called me! You're the one who wanted to come out for a drink tonight! And I never even asked you why." She pulls me into a tight hug. "I'm the worst. I'm so self-centered right now. The wedding has turned me into one of those Godzilla brides. I'm sorry."

"It's okay, it's fine. Don't sweat it."

"What was it all about? What were you needing a drink for? Tell me. I want you to."

"Meh. I don't know if it's worth dragging back up. It's just one of those things I have to deal with. I need to hike up my Big Girl panties and do it."

"What is it, though? Seriously. I want to know." Her eyes are a little glassy, her dark hair a little mussed, but she's sincere.

And I know she cares, of course. Still, I feel like I should protest. "I don't want to ruin the mood. We were having a good time."

She looks absolutely stricken, one hand over her heart. "Oh, my God. Is it something terrible? Is somebody sexually harassing you at work? No, wait, let me guess. Your boss wants you to go to dinner with that guy who called you just so you can make the sale. Right? I'll kill the bastard."

I shake my head, waving my hands to stop her before she tumbles off her stool while trying to find out where Rodney lives. "No, no, no, it's not that at all! Rodney doesn't even know Kent called, and he would never ask me to do something like that. Gross."

"Okay, good. Because I would've killed him."

I reach over to pat her hand. "I know. Honestly, it's nothing serious at all. When I'm not in the middle of the situation, it seems pretty stupid and petty. But when I'm in front of him, or he's running his stupid mouth…"

"Who?"

"Zack." I can't help but make a face before draining my glass.

"Zack. Okay. A coworker?"

I nod. "The worst. THE worst. He thinks he's God's gift to women, I swear. Walks around with his nose in the air, acting like he doesn't notice all the girls checking him out, but you know he does. You just know it. He's the type. I hate that type."

She nods slowly, thinking this over. "Yes. That does sound terrible."

"Don't patronize me," I warn. Considering that she calls me up, near tears, every time the slightest issue comes up with her wedding plans...

"I'm not patronizing you. I hate jerks like that, too. So what's his problem? And why is it your problem?"

"Rodney's making us work together on getting a house sold within a week. There's an open house this weekend that I'm hoping results in something solid, because I haven't come up with anything yet. And the clock's ticking."

"And you hate this guy you're working with?"

"You catch on fast." I grin.

"At least, it's only a week's worth of working with him. Right? I mean, that's good."

"My sister, the optimist," I groan. "Yeah, I guess that's good. But that's not the point, either. He's been doing everything in his power to steal this sale out from under me. He's lied to me about times for appointments, he's gone behind my back and scheduled showings without me. And I'm pretty damn sure he did something in there on Tuesday night, because when I took Mark in to see the place, it stank like rotten eggs. Though I'm still trying to figure out how he would've known about that, because I never told him I was bringing Mark around."

She takes this in, frowning. "Wait a sec. You're mad at him for scheduling a showing behind your back, but you just admitted that he wasn't supposed to know about you bringing Mark in to look around?"

My cheeks burn hot, and not because of the alcohol I just

finished. At least the lights are dim, so she can't see. "That's different."

"How?"

"Because he already lied to me about the appointment with the photographer and the seller, and he had already told me flat-out that I should step aside and give him the listing for himself."

My sister holds her head in her hands, wincing like she's in pain. "Wow. This is way too complicated. I almost wish I hadn't asked."

I nod vigorously, glad that someone else sees it the way I do. "And when I describe the whole thing to you, it sounds so childish. But I swear, when he's in front of me and his stupid mouth is moving and stupid things are coming out, I just want to…" I hold my hands up in front of me, like I'm gripping his neck with them, shaking them back and forth as I grimace.

"There's only one thing to do." She pulls out her phone. "What's his name? His full name?"

"Why?"

"I want to see if I can find him online. I need to get a look at him."

I lunge for her phone, but she pulls away before I can reach it. "Why, though? You're not going to leave him a nasty message on Facebook, are you?"

"How old do you think I am? Just because the two of you act like children…"

I know her well enough to know that she's not going to give

up easily. "Okay, wait. Hold on. I'll show you. His headshot and contact information are on the company website." It takes me no more than a few seconds to look it up, and I mime gagging as I hand my phone over with his picture expanded to fill the screen.

Her eyes bulge almost out of her head as she looks at the picture. "You have got to be kidding me. This is him? The terrible cretin you've been describing?"

"Yes, unfortunately. The anchor around my neck until we close on the house."

When she looks up at me, there's a wicked gleam in her eyes and her smile tells me I'm in for some serious teasing. "You. Are. So. Into. Him."

"False."

"True! You are! Oh, my God, you're practically ready to have his babies. It's so obvious. I didn't get it until I saw his picture, but now it's all coming together."

"Please. Get real!"

She thrusts the phone toward me. "Look at this man. Are you *looking* at him?"

"How can I not, with you shoving my phone in my face?"

She ignores me. "Look at those beautiful eyes. The hair—that dark, thick hair you just wanna bury your hands in. And that mouth! Oh, what I could do to that mouth!"

"Excuse me, but aren't you engaged?"

"What I would want that mouth to do to me!" She cracks an evil grin.

"Your fiancé's name is Luke, in case you forgot."

She only shakes her head. "Engaged ain't married, sis. I still know a gorgeous man when I see one."

"Just the same." I have to take the phone back before she drops it in my glass or goes even further into why Zack is worth cheating on her fiancé with. "Yes. I can admit he's good looking. Gorgeous, even. I'm not blind. But it's his attitude, like I said. You know as well as I do that a crappy attitude makes even the hottest guy ugly."

She grimaces, waving my protestations away. "Unless he's out there murdering kittens in front of small children and laughing over it, I can't imagine how he could ever be ugly."

"You'd be surprised."

"I still say you're into him," she insists.

"I still say you're drunk."

"Sienna and Zack, sittin' in a tree…" she sings, giggling as she fends me off when I slap her arms.

"Knock it off. I wish I had never told you about this."

She manages to stop laughing long enough to catch her breath. "He drives you nuts, doesn't he?"

I roll my eyes. "He pushes all my buttons."

"Do you drive him nuts, too?"

"I do my best," I admit. "Not proud of it, but it's the truth."

"And you like it when you piss him off, don't you?"

"Well, yeah. Because he deserves it."

She rests her chin on her palm, grinning like the Cheshire Cat. "Girl. You're so in lust with this guy, it's insane. I'm sorry. Deny it all you want. But you've presented me with the facts of the case and that's my verdict."

If I didn't have so much work to do tomorrow, I'd order another drink. "Thanks, Judge Judy. You're a lot of help."

# ZACK

I press my floor's number on the elevator panel, step back, and see Sienna walk through the entrance doors of the building. Her hair is in a high ponytail and she is wearing a sexy cream suit that does nothing to hide her curves. Her skin-tone high heels emphasis the tight muscles of her calves.

As the doors begin to swish shut our eyes meet across the foyer. Damn. I don't want to share the elevator with her. Let her take the next one.

Then…I see her slow down her pace, and I realize she doesn't want to share the elevator with me either. Bitch! I reach forward and hit the button that makes the doors open. Keeping my finger on the button I wait for her. I actually can't help the wolfish grin on my face.

For a second surprise flashes across her eyes, then she plasters a bright smile on her face and steps into the elevator.

The doors close and her perfume fills my nostrils. I find myself reacting to it. Fuck! I shouldn't have given in to that childish impulse to irritate her. I should have let her wait for the next elevator. I swing my gaze sideways and find her watching me. She's one of those women who looks great first thing in the morning.

"Good morning," I say.

She doesn't reply. Instead she steps forward and gently lays her finger on the red stop button. The elevator shudders to a sudden stop. She turns around and looks at me, her eyes full of something...hot. My throat goes dry. Did she just..?

I open my mouth to say, well God, knows what I wanted to say, but I would have thought of something.

"Don't talk, Zack," she interrupts. "In case you're wondering why I'm doing this, I should explain that a couple of things have been pissing me off." She nods at my surprised expression. "First off, I don't like the way you treat me."

Well, she sure didn't need to jam the elevator to tell me that.

"You treat me like a second-class citizen. From now on I want you to treat me like you do all the other women in our office."

My eyebrows rise. That's rich coming from her. She used to give me looks like I was the worst kind of pond scum. "In my defense, I thought you were too high and mighty to be treated like the other women."

"I'm not. Second, I think we both know that we can't carry on working closely until we eliminate whatever this thing is between us." She licks her lips and makes a backward and forward motion with her hand. "Perhaps if we just think of this clinically and just get this madness out of the way, everything will be fine. We'll be able to work without being distracted by...odd thoughts."

I can play along with the game. "And how do you propose to do that?"

She moves closer. So close I can smell her toothpaste. "Do I need to spell it out to you, Zack."

Not for my dick, she doesn't. It feels like it is on fire.

She touches my arm. "Do you know how wet I am for you?"

My eyes narrow. I'm not buying this. It must be some kind of trick. What the hell is she planning?

One eyebrow arches. "You don't believe me?"

"I'm sort of having a hard time reconciling this new brazenly sexual Sienna to the one who hates my guts."

"Oh, don't worry. I still hate you." Without taking her eyes off me she very clearly says, "But I just want you to fuck me, Zack. Hard. I need to get you out of my head and I don't know how else to do it. Just for today I am your malleable, obedient, slutty bimbo. Your fuck toy. Would you be able to fuck my cunt until I scream?"

I burned with lust at her words. God, I want her. Right here. Right now. Damn the consequences.

Slowly, she hitches her cream skirt up, over her knees, over her thighs, and over her hips. Jesus, she's not wearing panties. I stare at her freshly shaven pussy. Then she turns around, spreads her legs, and bends over with her palms planted on the mirrored doors of the elevator. The sight of her offering herself in such an obvious and slutty way is too much to bear. I stop thinking. Of their own free will my fingers slide into her glistening pussy.

"Yes," she gasps. Arching her back she pushes her hips

towards me so my fingers get shoved deeper into her hot cunt.

I don't have condoms on me, but I can't stop. Lust and hunger replace every rational thought. I have to have her. I have to. I unzip my trousers and release my dick from my boxers. It springs into action and I ram into her so power-fully she grunts. Hell, she feels exactly like what I thought she would. Hot and wet and tight. So fucking tight.

The relief of finally fucking the office queen bitch fizzles like bubbles through my veins. I've waited for this from the first moment she set her disapproving eyes on me. I'm going to make her scream my name until she's senseless. I pull out of her until only the head of my cock is still inside her them slam all the way in. Balls deep. I'm gonna show her

A buzzing sound filters through my fevered senses. For a second I don't recognize it.

"It's your phone. Are you going to answer it?" she asks.

"No," I growl.

With my cock still buried in her, she turns her head and looks at me calmly. "I think you should. It could be your wake-up call."

"What?"

Then I open my eyes. Light is filtering in through the curtains and my alarm clock is ringing. I roll over and stop it. "Oh shit," I groan, closing eyes against the light. Goddamn it, I should've known it was a fucking dream.

The elevator at work doesn't have a red stop button.

# SIENNA

O of. That fourth margarita might not have been the best decision I ever made.

Not that it matters how much my head is pounding because I'm always a professional no matter what. I flash my best smile to the couple to whom Zack and I are showing the house this morning. It's not their fault I drank too much last night, and on a work night, too. And for once, something isn't even Zack's fault.

What is his fault is the constant barrage of messages which have been hitting his phone since we got here. How unprofessional can a single person be? I wonder if he's going for a world record or something.

The Dawsons are completely oblivious to any of the drama swirling around them. They're a younger couple, late-30s at the oldest, and both far too interested in the house to notice the way I keep shooting daggers at Zack.

I suppose that's a good sign. They're so enamored with the house, they don't notice anything else. Not even the fact that one of the two realtors scheduled to show them the place keeps looking at his phone and even has gone so far as to step aside several times to answer messages.

It's like he doesn't care at all.

Which makes me wonder what those messages are all about. Who wouldn't?

"I love the spaciousness." Mrs. Dawson turns to me with wide eyes and an enthusiastic smile.

If I didn't know better, I'd say I have her on the hook. But I want to be cautious. I can't get cocky. "It's a dream, isn't it? The high ceilings, the large rooms. So much natural light, too." I look for Zack out of the corner of my eye, still smiling for the client's benefit. Where did he go?

Mr. Dawson, meanwhile, is in a happy world of his own. "I heard there's a media room?"

I can read him like a book. He's the type who'll have the boys over for football on his theater-style TV screen, where they can smoke cigars and be kings together.

"There sure is," I nod firmly. "Reclining theater seats, surround sound, massive screen. And soundproofed," I add with a glance at his wife, who shoots me a grateful look.

"I need to see this!" He turns and begins wandering off like he already owns the place.

My head swivels from side to side as I search for Zack. Where is he? "Zack? Mr. Dawson would like to see the media room."

"Already halfway there!" he calls out.

Then I hear him asking Mr. Dawson to join him moments later. I don't love the idea of the two of them speaking privately, without my being able to hear, but it means I can work my magic on the wife just as sure as the two of them can buddy it up and bond over sports.

"Everything is so perfect I'm almost afraid to see the kitchen. I've been let down before."

"I'm taking you there right now."

Mrs. Dawson beams at me. "Granted, I don't have time to do much cooking, but I love having a big kitchen where I can entertain guests while I am doing last minute touch ups."

"In that case, you'll love this." I show her around, reciting facts about the sub-zero refrigerator and butler's pantry, smiling and nodding in the right places as she explores the huge space. My brain isn't fully in the game, however, and not just because that third margarita is still a dull thud in my temples.

Mr. Dawson enters the kitchen like a man in a daze, and I can see that he's already mentally preparing for his big Super Bowl party. "It would be perfect for the awards show parties you throw for the girls," he informs his wife excitedly.

She laughs merrily. "Oh, yes, I'm sure you were thinking about me and the girls drinking champagne and eating hors d'oeuvres while you were in there. As if we just met."

I can't help but laugh with her. They seem to have a fun relationship, and I like working with couples who are relaxed enough to joke in front of me.

Zack should be laughing, too, even if he doesn't feel like

laughing, but Zack is not laughing because he isn't even in the room.

"Would you excuse me for a moment?" I duck out of the kitchen, still chuckling for their sake, but my face goes stony the second I'm out of there.

He's in the hall, eyes glued to his phone once again.

"What's up with you?" I hiss, waving. "I could use a little help in here."

Whatever is on his phone is clearly more important than to acknowledge my presence because he barely looks up. "I thought you were such a pro. That you could handle anything."

He. Is going. To die.

If my sister were here, I would point to this exact situation as case in point why there will never, ever be anything between Zack and me. She would see how off-base her jokes were if she could only see how utterly self-absorbed and petty he can be. I guess this is his way of punishing me, the jerk. I turn around without saying a thing and go back into the kitchen, my back stiff with disapproval.

"Sorry about that." I say as I wave the Dawsons back out to the entry, then upstairs. "You haven't seen anything until you've seen the master suite. The bathroom is to die for." One glance over my shoulder as I reach the hall tells me Zack is at the back of us, tapping furiously to create a message.

Who is he speaking with?

Another potential buyer?

That would make sense when combined with the way he seems so distant right now. He doesn't care how this showing goes because he's already got a client on the hook. Ooh, that would be so like him. It takes every ounce of self-control to continue with the showing as though there's nothing wrong. Even though I want nothing more than to take that phone of his and throw it out the window. I wonder if I could reach the lake from here.

As they're leaving, the Dawsons take turns shaking my hand, while Zack waits for them by their car.

"I have a good feeling about this." Mrs. Dawson grins, winking when her husband's not looking.

"So do I," I whisper with all the confidentiality of old girl-friends in cahoots with each other. She seems the type who would go for such a thing, and I honestly do like her. I'd feel good putting her in a house like this one. She'd make magic happen inside. She's one of those women I imagine whose fridges are always full. Unlike mine.

We chat over the next steps as we walk to their SUV, where Zack and Mr. Dawson are talking about football and Zack's reminding the client that he promised an invite to the first game once they're moved in and settled.

"Well, making plans already," I observe, noting the absence of Zack's phone. He's finally put it away. Now that the showing is finished.

"It's never too soon to plan for things like that." Mr. Dawson chuckles, clearly enjoying the visions of touchdowns, beer, and friends.

"Exactly. You wouldn't understand." Zack grins.

"It's nice seeing a couple work together, the way the two of you do," Mrs. Dawson observes as she climbs into the car.

Neither of us corrects her. What would be the point? We'd only look petty.

Once they've pulled away and it's just the two of us again, there's no need to play nice. Good thing, since pretending to like him is exhausting. "I guess I'll go in and make sure everything's turned off. You might as well leave since you're obviously not in the mood to do any work?"

"What's that supposed to mean?"

"Exactly what I said."

"Last time I checked, I was busy making nice with the husband while you chatted up the wife."

"You made nice when it suited you," I remind, striding through the house with him following behind me.

"God! It's impossible to please you! No matter what I do, there's something wrong with it."

"You poor baby," I sneer without looking back. "Maybe you should get on the phone and complain about me to whoever you were busy texting all throughout the showing. Maybe they'll care."

"Is that what this is about?"

He really is the densest person I've ever known. There's no other excuse for him to be so openly ignorant. I'm so furious, I can't even answer him. So I don't.

I was going to be a good girl. I told myself I would. I told myself it wasn't worth fighting with him, wasn't worth starting trouble, that we both clearly need this sale and I wouldn't be the one to ruin it. But when he's doing everything in his power to be a jerk, what am I supposed to do? Let him walk all over me?

Forget that.

"What about tomorrow?" he asks as I lock the front door.

My head isn't pounding as hard as it was, thank God, or else I'd really be unable to deal with his questions. What about tomorrow? What does he think? "What about it?" I ask, because I'll be damned if I'm going to give anything away about the open house.

"What's the game plan?"

"You're kidding, right? I wanted to talk with you about it yesterday, and you stalked off after insulting me. You lost your chance, buddy."

"You mean you're just going to commandeer the entire thing? Without consulting me?"

"Why would I consult you any further? Where has it gotten me so far?" I sweep past him on the way to the car, nails digging into my palms. The fact is, I'm not good at behaving this way. I've never outright fought with anyone except my sister, and that was only when we were kids. I'm usually the sort of person who cries when I get too emotional, even if that emotion is anger.

I'd die before I cry in front of him.

"You know what?" I ask when he doesn't offer a reply or even an explanation of his stupid, ignorant behavior during the showing. "Why don't you give up, just stop pretending you have any intention of sharing this listing with me, and ask to be reassigned? It's clear you don't intend on doing any work, and that you can't stand the sight of me." Whoa. Hang on. Where did that come from? I didn't mean to say that. But now it's out there, and there's no taking it back. I turn to face him because I have to. I can't slink away now.

His face is blank, unreadable.

And what does he do? Does he apologize? Does he assure me I'm wrong? Does he explain what all the phone nonsense was about?

No.

I might be able to forgive him if he at least tried to meet me halfway. I'll never forgive him for laughing. For straight-up laughing at me. He's still chuckling as I duck into my car and drive away, only after considering running him over before I go. Or at least clipping him.

Now that I'm alone, I can cry. And I do. Just a little—fine. A lot.

# SIENNA

"The hot hors d'oeuvres should be out on the island," I instruct one of the waitresses, pointing. "The backups can be left in the oven, I've set it to warm. Let's leave the extra champagne and juice on ice and make the mimosas as guests request them." I run through my mental checklist. "I know I don't need to tell you this, but I feel it bears mentioning: let's keep an eye on the repeat drinkers. We don't want anybody getting in an accident on the way home from here. We can set up a pick-up car for them, if need be."

I'm standing at the center of a hurricane as vendors make last-minute adjustments and I fire off instructions. There are small, tasteful floral arrangements strewn about, as well as a string quartet playing softly in the entryway. I adjust one of the arrangements, bringing it to the center of the side table it's sitting on, and remind myself to breathe.

Gosh, a mimosa sure would be great right now. I nearly have to slap my hand away when a uniformed butler passes through with a tray of them.

Zack wanders into the kitchen, and on his face, is a look I can only describe as a mix of admiration and sheepishness. He stops in front of me. "I'm impressed."

"Well. I guess my job is done then." I move to step around him and go someplace else, anywhere else, but he jukes to the side in time to block me.

"What is it with you? Why can't I even compliment you on a job well done without hearing your sarcasm?" His eyes are narrowed, troubled. Like he cares.

"I don't have time for this, Zack. If you'll excuse me." I manage to get past him this time and shake my head as I walk away, my heels clicking smartly against the marble floor in time with the kicky little tune the quartet is playing. There's a good energy in here today. I won't let anyone ruin it.

Not even my 'partner'

Before I know it, people start coming in. It's time to shine.

This is where I'm at my best—at least, in my opinion. Juggling people, their questions, making everyone feel welcome and valued. Making them feel at home. Encouraging without seeming pushing, which is a grave mistake so many realtors make.

Nobody wants to feel as though they're being stalked through a store, a house, anywhere money might eventually be changing hands. If anything, in my personal experience, a clingy salesperson is enough to change my mind and make me leave.

I don't make that mistake.

To my surprise, Zack is much more involved than he was yesterday. I don't get it. The Dawsons were practically on the hook, and talking about the house as though they were seriously considering the purchase. That was when he needed to be more involved, more personable, and available instead of staring at his phone like his whole life depended on it.

*I guess whoever he was making plans with ultimately fell through. He has to rely on what we manage to make happen today.*

It's a petty thought, but I can't help it. Pushing it away, I quickly turn my attention to the people walking through the door and answering their questions. There are a lot of questions, which is a terrific sign.

There are also a lot of compliments about the spread in the kitchen. I have to admit, the food smells fantastic, and it serves a purpose beyond making the guests feel pampered. The scent leads them to the kitchen, where they have a reason to slow down and look around. The kitchen is a big selling point in any house, and this kitchen is an absolute showplace.

By the time two hours pass, my legs are burning from going up and down the stairs so many times. This is better than a trip to the gym, and ultimately better for my bank account.

Zack is in the library, answering questions about the square footage.

Once he's alone, I wave him over. He looks nearly jubilant. I can tell he loves this as much as I do, the sense that our buyer is somewhere in the house and we're invisibly reeling them in.

I hate to burst his bubble. "I'm going to have to leave you to it for the last half hour," I murmur, straight-faced.

His eyes widen. "What? You know this is the busiest time."

He's not wrong, either. There are still at least a dozen couples walking through the house, some of whom have been here for a while. They're pretty serious too.

"You can handle it. I have some other things to take care of. The vendors know what to do once things wind down. I've already given them detailed instructions."

He blinks, silent for a long moment. "Fine. Go."

I manage a tight smile for the sake of the people nearby. "I wasn't asking permission. I thought I'd do you the favor of letting you know you'd be on your own, is all." I wish I didn't relish the way he struggles to conceal his irritation, but it just feels so good.

I ought to feel bad for leaving him on his own. I know I should. There are still plenty of interested people with plenty of questions for us, but there are things I need to take care of. Things he doesn't need to know about.

It's not like a half-hour is going to kill him. He's been coasting throughout this week. A little hard work, a little hustle, will be good for him.

# SIENNA

Hours later, we're in the same house, but we may as well be on another planet. The backdrop has changed that much. This is my biggest move, the one that always results in either a sale or at least a ton of new connections. And *Zack* has no idea, which is the best part of all.

"Okay, ladies!" I hold up my martini glass, signaling for quiet. I recognize many of the faces around me but there are at least a half-dozen strangers, which is very good. Fresh meat.

And maybe new friends, too. That's always nice.

"To a lovely evening in a fabulous house," I toast, clinking my glass with a few of the other women around me. "Now, manis and pedis have been set up in the library; and makeup and hair in the family room. We have a double feature in the media room: *Notting Hill* and *The Notebook*." I learned a while back no matter how tough a woman is in the boardroom, she can appreciate a bit of romance on her night off. "You know where to find the drinks and food. The kitchen's fully stocked, but please feel free to ask for anything that seems to be running low. I know I'll be scarfing down the mini egg rolls, so hands off."

Everybody laughs before dispersing, moving to the areas they're interested in. The chatter is encouraging. I've never had a martini go down so smooth before. I deserve it after all the hard work I've put into this evening. It's not just my male clients that I understand. I understand women too, having been one all my life. And I know there's nothing more fun than a night spent with the girls and they appreciate the chance to relax.

I always encourage my longtime friends and favorite clients to bring friends with them, especially if they're friends I've never met before. These are some seriously kickass women here, investment geniuses, CEOs, Presidents and I know that at least two of them are seriously looking for a trophy home.

I think what I enjoy the most about nights like this - aside from the chance to sell a house, of course - is the fact that I can be myself around them. I don't have to tone myself down or make myself smaller in order to protect their egos. I don't have to pretend to be someone I'm not, just to come off as likeable.

Though I do my best to be likeable, obviously.

"Laughter sounds good in this house," I observe with a smile, walking into the room where five women are sitting at portable manicure stations with their feet soaking.

Crystal, a past client I've stayed in close touch with over the years, sips from her Chablis before agreeing. "I was just commenting on how perfect this house is for big holiday parties. Can you imagine? It would be spectacular."

Oh, thank God for her. I might have to send her flowers for that little comment. She knows just how to help me out. "You're so right. Every time I step through the front door, I imagine what a gigantic Christmas tree would look like under the chandelier." I leave the room on that note, letting the girls imagine for themselves.

The hair and makeup room is much the same, with giggling filtering out into the hall. "Anybody need a refill in here?" I ask, poking my head in the door.

"Why don't you come in and relax a little with us?" Melissa, another old friend and client says. One of my first sales, now that I think about it.

"Is this your way of nicely telling me I need a makeover?" I ask with a wink.

"Please!" she shouts over the chorus of laughter which has erupted. "I should be so in need of a makeover. You look like you just walked off a film set. Do you even have pores?"

I'm about to make a joke at my own expense, but something interrupts me. Yup, the utter darkness the house plunges into when the power goes out.

"No flipping way," I whisper to myself before raising my voice to be heard. "It's all right, I'm sure it's just a blown fuse. No problem! I'll go out and check the fuse box."

Meanwhile, the words running through my head aren't quite so calm or confident. What the hell is this? Why tonight? Why right now? My best-case scenario would be a blown fuse.

The worst? I don't even want to think about it. I went to too much trouble for things to go south so early in the evening.

Using my phone as a flashlight, I step out through the back door and walk around to the side of the house, where I know the fuse box is located inside an attached tool shed. It's full darkness out here, moonless, without even many visible stars.

I don't need a moon to be able to see what's pulling away, off by the woods at the edge of the property.

A sports car. A rather splashy one. A car which has no business being here right now and whose driver seems to be in an awful hurry to get away.

Zack. Damn him to hell.

How did he find out? He didn't really need to be sneaky about it. He could've just shown up to check on things and found us. The dick.

And sure enough, all that needs to be done to bring the lights back is flipping the breaker. He's so basic in his sabotage. Did he imagine being a girl, I wouldn't know how to flip a switch. Now, I'm more certain than ever that he did something to make the house stink the night I brought Mark over. How juvenile can he be?

My hand reaches for the breaker.

I stop myself just before flipping it.

Maybe there's another way.

"I knew I remembered seeing a million candles in the basement." I chuckle on lighting the last of the many the girls helped me set up in the library. "Mani/pedi by candlelight. I only regret that we can't show the movies now." There were only two or three women in there at the time the power went out, anyway. Most everyone was more interested in a night of beauty.

We've moved everything to the library, which is more than big enough for all of us, and even though the hair stylists can't do their blowouts, they can still create classy up-do's and fun, cute styles the women all seem to love.

The room is absolutely gorgeous with the light from the candles flickering off the walls while the mood is cozy, warm and full of girl talk. If anything, it's better than before.

Best of all…it looks like I handled the situation with panache and grace, and that I know how to make lemonade out of a pile of lemons. All of this is working in my favor.

I ought to send flowers to Zack, too, while I'm ordering an

arrangement for Crystal. Wouldn't that burn him up? I won't even explain why. I'll just send a "thank you" card with them.

The thought makes me smile as the girls gossip about their work and their men, and in some cases how long it's been since they've gotten any. I know how that goes—boy, do I—but I can't speak up. Unprofessional. I settle for smiling and nodding, laughing in the right places, answering questions about the house as they come my way.

And sipping another martini. Because I deserve it.

Crystal catches my eye and points to one of the girls, who happens to be walking toward me. Her name is Faye, I remember, and she's one of Crystal's friends. An interior designer with her own thriving business and a very rich boyfriend. "Do you have a second?" she whispers.

"Of course. What can I do for you?"

"I just wanted to let you know that I'm very interested," she murmurs with a smile. "We're all having so much fun, I almost hate to break it up by talking about business."

"But that's also what we're here for." I grin. "I mean, ulti-mately. I wanted everyone to see this place, because it's incredible. I want it to go to a nice person, especially someone who will know what to do with it. Because it has so much potential."

Her eyes go round. "Oh, I've been imagining for an hour now how I would decorate it!"

There's so much giggling going on, including between Faye and me, that I almost miss the sound of the front door open-ing. A latecomer? No, it's far too late for that.

My heart sinks when one, then two male voices ring out in the entryway. I should've seen this one coming. Why didn't I?

"What's going on in here?" Zack steps into the library, all smiles, followed by an almost supernaturally tall man who I think might be a professional basketball player. If he's not, he ought to be.

Zack must feel the weight of my stare—more like a glare—because he turns to me right away. "What happened? No power?"

This dick. This unfathomable dick. "No, we're fine." I smile broadly. "Just a little flub with the fuse box. But it gave me the idea to set up the candles, and we've been having a great time."

His face darkens a bit, but that might just be a trick of the candlelight as it flickers. Then, he smiles. "That's nice. I'm glad to know my friend and I can walk through with no trouble."

But his friend doesn't seem to care much about the house anymore. He's more interested in the nearly two dozen women hanging out around the library—and they are interested right back, whispering and nudging each other and making eyes at him like they just got back from several years on a desert island.

Not surprising, they're even more interested in Zack. I bite my tongue before I have the chance to tell them not to stroke his ego. He doesn't need any help with that.

"Hello, ladies." He grins, his voice warm and friendly. Naturally, he's picked up on the energy in the room.

God, I hate him so much.

"I didn't know boys were allowed to this party," Faye murmurs, raising an eyebrow.

I want to wave my arms in front of her face and remind her of what we were just discussing before the interruption. I fear the moment is gone and I need to find a way to rope her in again, but it won't be possible while she's looking Zack up and down like he's a slice of juicy steak.

"Technically, there aren't," I manage to growl through clenched teeth.

"I would've steered clear had I know there was a party," Zack points out.

His smile is a little too tight, but something tells me I'm the only person who notices. The ladies are too busy being dazzled by the outer package to pick up on what's going on between us. "Something tells me you wouldn't have," I hiss at the back of his head as he allows Crystal and one of the others to usher him further into the room, offering him the food and drink I worked so hard to bring together. How does he keep managing to do this? How does he always come out on top, or close to it?

I was so close to getting Faye on the hook, too. Now, she's peppering Zack's tall buddy with questions about his life while shooting longing looks in Zack's direction. Looks like she's forgotten all about her boyfriend. Meanwhile, Zack is busy fending off no fewer than three of the girls, all of whom are feeling sassy and sexy thanks to new makeup and too much wine.

And oh, he's lapping it up like a dish of cream. That's the worst part of all. It's not enough that he ruined my girl's night. Now, he has to spike the ball by flirting shamelessly. If

I hear him mention one more time how lucky he is to be in the middle of so many beautiful ladies, I'll throw up.

I might make sure to be close to him when I do, too. He deserves it.

It's a relief when things start to wrap up a half hour later. I feel unfulfilled, let down, though Faye did promise to call me in the morning. Maybe she'll be able to focus when Zack isn't around. I wish I were as lucky as her, with the chance to leave and never see him again. I air kiss them all goodbye and close the door.

# SIENNA

"Need some help?" Zack asks as I begin cleaning up. He leans against the wall by the door, hands in the pockets of his jeans. Even in casual clothes, he looks like a million bucks. The candlelight is so not helping matters. He looks sexy. Smoldering.

"You've helped more than enough, thanks," I mutter, turning my back to him so I won't have to see him anymore. There are too many conflicting opinions battling for domination in my head and other parts of my body somewhat further south.

"At least let me go out there and turn on the lights."

I manage to snort instead of screaming. "You ought to know how it's done, since you're the one who turned them off."

"It was a dirty trick you pulled. You left me here today, and for what? So you could plan this for tonight?"

"What about it?" I demand, tossing a handful of crumpled

napkins into a garbage bag. "Like you haven't done anything dirty to me. Nice stink bombs, by the way."

He lets this roll off his back, like he expected me to figure out it was him.

Gee, does he actually respect my intelligence? Or maybe he wanted me to know. I wouldn't be surprised.

"That's what you get for going behind my back."

"Like you did with Kent, you mean?" I offer my nastiest smile. "Is selling this house on your own really that important to you? Or is winning all that really matters?"

"I could ask you the same question."

"Listen up." I drop the bag on the floor, hands on my hips. "Let's finish this now. You're the one who set the tone in this arrangement by telling me to dump the listing."

"I didn't tell you to do anything," he argues. "I suggested."

"Bullshit," I snarl. "I was ready to be professional. Civil. To work with you. You're the one who started this, and now you have the nerve to get mad at me for turning the tables on you. Maybe you'll remember how it sucks to be on the receiving end of that sort of treatment the next time you want to work your wiles on a woman."

"Is that what this is about?" he asks, eyebrows almost shooting up off his forehead.

"What?"

"Working my wiles?" He chuckles, stepping away from the wall. "Did you think I was flirting with you? Did you expect more where that came from? And now you're disappointed?"

"No! Don't make me laugh. All I meant was, you thought you could muscle me out of it. Then, you thought your charm would do the trick. Sorry to disappoint you, but I'm not as naïve as the women you charmed tonight."

"Look who's talking!" He laughs, coming closer, fists still jammed in his pockets. He blinks rapidly, fluttering his eyelashes. "Oh, Kent, you're so funny!" he coos, sarcasm dripping from his voice.

"I never once said that."

He drops the imitation, sneering. "Maybe not in so many words, but don't pretend you didn't use what you have to your advantage as you tried to steal my client. Didn't work so well for you, did it?"

"I don't know. If I hadn't turned him down when he asked me to dinner, things might have gone a lot better."

He frowns, but only for a moment. "He asked you to dinner?"

"Yes. And I turned him down, because I have principles. In case you didn't know."

"Huh." He nods, his eyes moving over me before a slow smile spreads over his face. "It's not a surprise, though. I would never expect you to go through with the show you put on."

I swear, I can't explain why that comment or that taunting grin makes my blood boil even if there was a gun to my head and somebody demands I figure it out. All I know is, I want to slap him for it. I know I should walk away. Not dignify that silly remark, but I can't. "Why not? You think I'm made of stone? You think I'm not woman enough to follow up on what I hint at?"

"Something like that," he murmurs, taking another step my way.

My heart is pounding so hard, so fast, I can barely breathe. It's rage... so I tell myself. It couldn't possibly be the fact that we're now only a few feet from each other and the flickering glow of the candles makes him look sexier and more mysterious than I've ever seen him. Or the way he stares at me, his eyes hooded to conceal his expression, his lips so tempting...

"You're wrong," I breathe. "You don't know me at all."

"No," he agrees, closing the gap between us.

I can feel the heat coming from his body, which is almost touching mine.

"I don't know you. And I can't decide if that's a good thing, or..."

My breath catches. "Or?"

"Or if I want to know everything about you. *Every last thing.*"

I don't have time to think or even move before he takes my face in his hands and pulls me to him, crushing our mouths together. There's no tenderness in his kiss, no hesitation. We're like two cars colliding, smashing into each other, tearing each other apart.

My fingers turn into claws which grip his shoulders—so firm, so thick—before my arms wind around his neck. I'm not just holding onto him, keeping him close as our mouths move together and he kisses me until it almost hurts. I'm holding myself up, because my legs are too weak to support me.

His arms close around my back, pulling me, pressing my

body to his from head to toe and I lean into him. Oh God, yes! Yes, this is what I need. I need his hands stroking my back, I need his tongue sweeping slowly along the inside of my mouth. I need the fire growing in my core as his muscles move under my hands—shoulders, arms, back, all of it so warm and hard.

Hard like what's pressing against my thigh as we sink to the floor, his excitement as evident as mine, as hard as the floor under my back, as I stretch out under him, our breaths coming in short gasps as his hands slide under my sweater. One of them cups my breast as his mouth trails warm, wet kisses down my throat. I'm totally lost, fingers tangling in his hair, his name coming from my mouth again and again in a hoarse whisper, "Zack…oh, Zack…"

"So fucking sweet," he groans, thrusting his hips against me and driving his hard length into my thigh.

It sends shivers down my spine and making the heat between my thighs burn hotter. As hot as the flames of the candles burning all around us.

I can't believe this is happening. But it was always going to, wasn't it? Yes, and this is the perfect place. It makes sense, doing it here, the place which brought us together. I wrap a leg around his, my skirt riding up, my body writhing of its own accord, moving toward what it wants most. Him. All of him, all over me.

*Bzzz, bzzz.*

For a second there' blankness. Then words filter into the emptiness of my brain. His phone. In his pocket.

My eyes fly open and I see this for what it really is. I'm on a bare floor, beneath him, my sweater pushed up around my neck and his lips against the swell of one of my breasts. Both of us panting like animals. One of his thick thighs is jammed between mine. I was seconds away from grinding against his leg, just to get a little satisfaction.

Horror washes over me.

"Oh, God," I mutter, pushing him away.

He moves easily, silently, not bothering to fight, clearly as stunned as I am.

I can't look at him. I can't give him time to ask what just happened and why I'm running away because oh, my God, I wouldn't know what to say. I'm so ashamed.

Humiliated.

I run out of there like a bat out of hell. It isn't until I'm in the car, driving away—hoping he decides to finish cleaning up the place and knowing, somehow, that he will—that I realize he probably did that just to throw me off even further. There's no other explanation.

Is there?

# SIENNA

I wish I were dead. Not just sick or in a coma. Flat-out dead.

How am I supposed to face him after what happened last night? I can hardly face myself.

One minute I was in control, cleaning up after what could've been a successful night if it weren't for him, and the next I was writhing around on the floor like a horny teenager making out for the first time. Ugh. I cringe anew. This is a complete mess.

Now he knows… what does he know? That I think he's hot. That his sexiness does indeed affect me no matter how hard I've worked to convince him otherwise. He knows he's got the upper hand…or, at least, what he'll see as the upper hand.

Because I was so into it. I was *so, so* into it. It never even crossed my mind to try and stop him when he kissed me. Oh, no, quite the opposite. I nearly tore his clothes to pieces. Ugh! I close my eyes at the horror.

At least it's a Sunday, and there shouldn't be anybody else in the office. I need to be here instead of at home if I hope to get anything done at all. Otherwise, it would be impossible to resist the awful prospect of staying in bed and endlessly replaying the X-rated movie starring Zack and me from last night.

My to-do list isn't insurmountable, not by a long shot. I dive into it with the intention of using work to wipe away memories of last night. I have to follow up with Faye. I have to shoot Crystal a message and thank her for introducing us. I have to order little gifts to thank my clients for coming over. Nothing big, nothing that might embarrass them. Just something to let them know I appreciate their time.

*Ding!*

The elevator bell chimes, signaling the arrival of someone new to the floor. What are the odds? It could be anybody, anyone else at all. Even a member of the maintenance crew. Please God, let it be anybody, but Zack. Please, please.

But of course, it isn't. Why would it be? Has anything else gone my way over the course of this entire situation?

My door is open, so Zack sees me when he walks past. And I see him. It's a real struggle to keep my head held high, like I didn't do anything last night which might have mortally humiliated me.

"Hey," he says by way of greeting, sounding surprised, but not the least bit embarrassed or awkward. He probably rolls on the floors of empty houses with women all the time. "What are you doing here?"

"I had some work to get done," I report as cheerfully as possible, keeping my eyes on the screen in hopes that he won't notice my burning face. Why did it have to be him? Why can't I stop thinking about what an all-around excellent kisser he is?

"Same here," he murmurs. Instead of walking away, as I hoped and prayed he would, he steps inside my cubicle.

Because why not? I'm already near death by humiliation, so why not push me over the edge?

"I guess it's a good idea for us to talk over a few things."

Oh, God, just take me now. Please. I'll miss my family and it stinks that I won't be around for the wedding, but I'm fairly sure that it will be for the best this way. I fumble around for the best, most noncommittal thing to say. "What do you have on your mind?"

"Well, Rodney expected us to have a buyer by the end of the day. I just don't think that's possible."

I blink, waiting for more. Could it be that he truly only wants to discuss work? Okay. I can handle that. I swivel around in my chair until I'm facing him. His expression is neutral. I can't say he's not thinking about last night, but it doesn't look as though he's letting it color what we're talking about right now. And that's a relief. I think. Is he really that unfazed by what happened last night?

"I agree," I admit, leaning back in my chair. "It's one thing to get people interested in a house, but another to get them to commit to a price tag such as this in only a few days. No matter how wealthy, these clients are savvy enough to view such a purchase as a major investment. They want to be careful about it."

"I think Nick would be understanding of that, although Rodney would be the best person to broach the subject with him."

"Also agreed." I have to smile a little. A genuine smile. He's smart. And he's being very mature about last night. Maybe I was wrong, maybe it wasn't just a power play on his part. I've been wrong before. I can admit it.

"But we do have several very interested leads," he adds, raising an eyebrow.

"Oh, sure thing. There's Faye, and a couple of the other women who viewed the place last night." I swallow quickly, hoping to push past the lump that forms in my throat at the thought of lying on the floor with him, surrounded by candles. "And the Dawsons, for sure. I say we reach out to them today to follow up before too much time passes."

"I can do that," he offers.

I wish I didn't feel like I have to hesitate and consider everything he says from more than one angle, but I still do. What would he have to gain by approaching them on his own? They would more than likely ask what happened to me? I think so…I made enough of an impression on them. And if I suddenly dropped off the sale, they'd have to wonder what happened and whether they want to go through with it. At the very least, it would slow up the sale. He can't afford to make that sort of mistake right now.

It seems safe enough, I guess. "All right. Thanks. Let me know what they say."

"Of course, I would. And you let me know what Faye thinks."

I scowl inwardly. Faye was supposed to be my client, damn it, which he's very well aware of no matter how innocent he tries to look. "Sure thing," I reply, sounding as cool as possible under the circumstances.

I can't help but jump when his phone buzzes, not just out of surprise, either. It's a reminder of what happened last night, and how embarrassing it was for me.

He even looks somewhat apologetic when he reaches for the device. When he sees whatever is on the screen, his expression changes. "Oh. I have to deal with this. Sorry." He doesn't even look at me as he turns to walk away. I no longer exist.

"Hang on a second...!" But it's too late. He is so freaking rude, and it's like he doesn't get it at all. Or, he just doesn't care.

"Obviously, I don't rank as important enough for him to finish a conversation with," I huff, crossing my arms. He's already on the other side of the floor, down by Rodney's empty office. I wonder why he didn't simply go to his cubicle. Maybe because the office is closer to the elevators, and he's planning on making a quick getaway based on the outcome of his call.

When I poke my head out through the doorway, I catch sight of him. "No, he did not just go into Rodney's office and shut the door to take his goddamned call," I mutter in mixed surprise and disgust. Who the hell does he think he is? And what's so important that he needs to close himself in, so I can't hear him?

Is he talking to another secret client? Son of a bitch, I'd bet anything that he is. That's why he's being so secretive, so I won't figure it out. Does he think I'm that stupid? What? Just because we made out last night, he thinks I'll overlook this new round of sketchy behavior? He has another thing coming.

While his back is still turned, I shift my attention to his laptop bag that he left on the floor, just inside my cubicle. It's open, and the flashing lights coming from the machine inside tell me it's on.

Should I?

No. I shouldn't.

But I want to.

It wouldn't ruin his entire life. He could still get his work done, but only on his phone and nowhere else. He might even be able to get his data back. Maybe.

I can't believe I'm sliding the laptop from the bag, all the while making sure he's not watching. I can't believe I'm opening it, rolling my eyes when the desktop immediately pops up. He doesn't even bother to lock it.

If anything, he deserves what's about to happen. I'm only teaching him a lesson on the value of the lock screen.

While keeping an ear out for his exit from Rodney's office, I do what needs to be done. We'll see how efficient he is with a freshly-wiped computer.

ZACK

"**D**amn her."

Just when I think we're on solid footing, she goes and pulls a stunt like this. After last night, I was sure we turned a corner. I wanted to comfort her, or at least tell her there was nothing to get so freaked out about, but she ran out of there like all the hounds of hell were after her, and I couldn't leave a million burning candles unattended.

And now she's run out on me again. That's the part that disappoints me most. She did something to my laptop and fled before I could catch her. It's the only explanation. The damn thing was working just fine earlier, before I left for the office. Now, I get the start-up desktop I got when I first bought the thing.

She's managed to restore factory settings on it. I can't even log in with my own username and password. They're not recognized.

Stupid me, thinking I could leave it lying around. Thinking she was better than pulling a bullshit move like this.

All right. Even I can admit, she's pretty clever.

So maybe I deserve it a little bit for doing what I did to her. Turning out the lights wasn't one of my better moves. Then again, she's the one who held a party without my knowledge. Tit for tat, or so it seemed at that time.

Now?

Now, I can't stop thinking of her on the floor underneath me, and if I'll ever get my files back.

I reach for the phone, automatically thinking about calling her, but no. That would just make things worse. We'll end up getting into one of those circular arguments we seem to be so skilled at, running around each other, throwing blame. And no matter how long we go at it, it doesn't make a bit of difference. It sure doesn't solve anything.

Instead, I call Rodney. I need to give him an update, anyway. I'll let him know something's happened to my laptop. It will help if he gets on my case about how slowly we're progressing with the sale.

"Working on a Sunday?" He chuckles.

"If I didn't work on a Sunday, I wouldn't be me," I say easily.

"I hope you're calling with good news."

I don't miss a beat. "Well, this isn't the best news I've ever shared with you."

"Uh-oh. What happened?"

"Somehow, my laptop wiped itself and restored to factory settings. The only work I can do right now is through my phone."

"You're kidding! What happened? Something fried your drive? A power surge?"

"Yeah, I don't know. I'm looking into it as we speak. I can always hook up with the cloud and get my files back, but that'll take a while. And I need to find my mailbox on the network, too." My fingers tap the keys absently. "I'm afraid my contact list may be gone. I might be able to sync my phone up, but it'll all take time."

"I hope so. I'd hate to see you lose all that data."

"No kidding. So listen, about the listing…"

"Now, we get to the real point of the call," he replies.

"Everything's fine, progressing well, but I just spoke with Sienna about it and we agree that the week-long timeline wasn't reasonable. Not that we're complaining," I continue, cutting him off when I can tell he's about to protest. "We have at least two, maybe three very serious contenders here. But we're also talking about a multi-million-dollar sale. The clients are exercising caution. You know how counterproductive pushing too hard is."

"I do."

"We just need a few more days to massage a decision out of one of them. That's all. We're nearly in the home stretch. Would it be possible to speak with Nick?" Meanwhile, I'm struggling to even populate my inbox with emails I know are there. Damn her for setting me back like this.

"I'll see what I can do. I agree, the notion of securing a buyer within a solid week was a bit unrealistic, but clients don't understand the ins and outs."

"No, they don't. I really appreciate it. I'm reaching out to one of the interested parties today, while Sienna reaches out to another."

"How are things going between you two?"

My fist clenches. Strange. I don't even like the idea of discussing her with him. "Pretty well. I can see how she's gotten as far as she has." That's a fair and professional summation of her. No matter what I do to slow her down or downright stop her, she simply ups her game in response.

He laughs. "I knew she'd be the perfect match for you."

"You generally do know best." And now I'm just flat-out kissing his ass, but what the hell? We chat for a few more minutes before I hang up, and I get back to trying to undo the damage she's done.

I'm too busy trying to salvage my computer while remembering what happened last night to notice the texts coming in on my phone, but when I do, I groan at the caller ID.

Jenny…air hostess.

I would normally not be in a bad mood at the sight of her name. Especially, considering she's asking if we can hang out tonight. We get together like this every few weeks or so when she's in town, and it's never a bad time. We both know the score. We're friends with benefits.

Only I'm not in the mood. Which is unusual for me. Unheard of, even.

I glance down at my crotch, where all evidence points to the contrary. And I realize something…it's not that I'm not in the mood. It's that I'm not in the mood for Jenny. Because as I've been sitting here, I've been remembering last night and the way Sienna's lips tasted. The feel of her body under my hands. The smoothness of her skin and the way she arched her back and burst into flames when I touched her. The way her entire body reacted to my slightest touch.

If I were honest, it was always inevitable that we'd end up on that floor together. If anything, I'm surprised it took as long as it did.

Being with Jenny - sexy as she is - wouldn't measure up after even a few minutes on a bare hardwood floor with Sienna, both of us fully dressed. In fact, I can't think of a single person who would measure up after that. I type out a text reply.

*Not tonight. At the office, not sure when I'll even be free. Sorry.*

Hell, I just passed up getting laid. And this is not even the first time. I did it last week at the club when that blonde came on to me too. All because of the woman who breaks my balls for sport and just ruined my computer.

But somehow, I feel like it is the right decision.

# SIENNA

Hmmm… what's his angle now?

He must know it was me who messed up his machine and yet, he hasn't let on. My conscience has been bugging me terribly for the rest of the yesterday and well into this morning. I don't know why he has this effect on me. I become such an idiot when he's around. I wonder if he managed to get things working again. Knowing him, he did. Nothing ever affects him for long.

He's made of Teflon or something.

I've walked up and down the hall so many times, it's amazing that I haven't worn a rut into the floor. He's in there with Rodney. I hate feeling this way, like a little girl who's afraid her brother will tattle to Daddy. But what else could they be talking about in Rodney's office? Why can't I be part of their conversation?

What is he telling Rodney about me? About us?

Becca gets up from her desk, just outside Rodney's office,

and notices me glancing her way. "What's up?" she whispers, eyes twinkling like we're in cahoots.

"Nothing. Just wondering what's going on in there. We still don't have a contract for any of our prospects. Zack was going to talk to Rodney about that." It's partly true, at any rate. I'm still concerned about the amount of time it's taking to get the job done. That last thing either of us needs is for Nick to pull us out of the sale because we haven't held up our end of the bargain.

"I did overhear Zack mention a showing tonight, and how confident he is about it. That seemed to make Rod happy."

The news is like a lead weight in my gut. "Right. The showing." The showing Zack magically forgot to tell me about. So that's what his call was about yesterday. I knew it. He was plotting behind my back. I realize I'm shaking...

Then Becca sees my trembling. "Are you okay? I think you're working too hard. You look exhausted." She puts a hand to my forehead, frowning.

"I'm fine. Just tired. You're right. I'm just tired. I think I'll go home for a little while, try to get some rest. If Rodney asks, can you let him know?"

Becca nods and shoos me to my desk, where I gather my things and head for the door, still in a daze.

I could kill him. What is it with this guy? Why is he so determined to shut me out of this sale? And how dare he act like I'm the problem when he keeps going behind my back? A single tear spills onto my cheek, which I brush away with impatience. Now isn't the time to get emotional.

It's time to get even.

In another half hour, I'm finished placing mouse traps all over the house and not in discreet, out-of-the-way places, either. All throughout the kitchen, beside the fridge, sticking out from under the stove, in the pantry, on the counters. We'll see what his private client thinks about this when they arrive. Then I go to have dinner with my sister.

---

"I swear, lady, you are going to make sure I don't fit into my wedding gown," Tami says with a laugh.

I eye up my sister as she folds a slice of pizza and takes a huge bite. "Nobody's forcing you to eat a slice as big as your head."

She makes a face. "I can't help that it's so good."

"It is good," I have to admit. "So, did you finalize the design of the invitations? The printer's going to need them within a week, two at the most."

"I think so. Every time I'm sure I've made my mind up, I have second thoughts. I just need to choose one and stick to my guns."

"What's Luke think?" I ask, though I know the answer before she speaks.

"Please." She snorts, shaking her head. "All he knows is the day the wedding's taking place. That's about the most I can get him to pay attention to." He's a great guy, but definitely the type to shut down in the face of so many details.

"Hey. You."

We both look up in time to find Zack storming over to our

table. How in the world did he know I would be here? Unless he found a way to look at my calendar. Is it possible?

His nostrils are flared and I'm fairly sure his eyes are about to shoot fire by the time he reaches us. I take note of his clenched fists as I smile coolly up at him. "Hey! Are you hungry? This place has great pizza."

"Give me a break," he snarls. "I just wanted to come in and thank you for the presents you left in the kitchen. Very classy."

I shrug, as blank faced as I can be, though it's a different story inside. Inside, I don't know if I should laugh, or be a little worried about him. I might have gone too far this time. He looks like he could blow his top at any moment. "I was concerned about the presence of mice in the house. Or maybe it was rats. You know, I'm not very good at telling the difference."

"Enough." It's a hiss, low and dangerous. "Are you ever going to get tired of playing these ridiculous games?"

I stand, never breaking eye contact or even blinking. "Are you ever going to get tired of scheduling showings behind my back?" Then, I smile again. "You look a little flustered, Zack. And your face is so flushed. I'm worried about you. Maybe the stress is getting to be a bit too much. I think it's time for you to step aside and give me the listing, if you can't handle the pressure."

He holds my gaze for a beat before sneering, almost laughing, then turning his back on me and walking away.

I watch, still standing, until he's out the door. Only then can I sit down, my knees shaking.

"Whoa. So that's Zack," Tami breathes.

I almost forgot she was sitting opposite me. "Yes. Sorry I didn't get the chance to introduce you."

She takes a handful of napkins and fans herself. "I don't know about you, but it feels to me like the temperature just jumped twenty degrees in here."

"Maybe because my head almost burst into flames," I suggest.

"Or maybe because the two of you are so ridiculously into each other," she whispers.

"Once again, shut up. That's not how it is. You just watched us together. We hate each other."

"Right. That's why it seemed for a second there like you were about to suck each other's faces off."

"You have such a descriptive way with words." I wince as I reach for my ice water. I need to cool down. How does he always do this to me?

"Honey, just admit it. You're nuts for him. Your chemistry is off the charts. I mean, I could literally feel the fire between you guys. I almost felt guilty for sitting here, like I should've left you alone."

"Knock it off."

"I mean it!" She laughs…then, with a sigh she asks, "Did you really put out mouse traps in the kitchen?"

I reach for another slice. "Don't judge me. You don't know the whole story."

"So tell me," she invites with a big-assed grin.

# SIENNA

"Are you freaking serious?" I blurt out when I see the pile of unanswered emails about the house. I can't believe he hasn't responded to any of these emails.

Oh. Wait. Yes, I can believe it, because that's the sort of thing he excels at: pretending to be a hard worker who just wants to do a good job, then ditching anything resembling work when he really needs to buckle down and do it.

Hypocrisy, thy name is Zack.

Hang on. Let me just check that he's getting them, too. Yes, we're both included on the list of recipients. Why hasn't he sent a single reply? Does he think people like the ones we're dealing with have the patience to deal with bullshit like his?

No. It's a message to me. And he acts like I'm the childish one.

Fine, then. I'll answer all these email on my own and...I'll handle the showing at noon on my own too. He doesn't need to know a thing about it.

"Oh, shoot." I'm running late for it, too. I wanted to get there before the clients, just in case he left a surprise for me the way I did for him.

How far we've both fallen. I shouldn't have sunk to his level in the first place.

Too late now. I shove my arms into my coat and make sure to shut down my laptop. Don't want to fall for my own tricks, now, do I? If I could just tip-toe out of my cubicle and down the hall without anyone seeing me and I don't get stuck having to answer questions, I'll be good.

No such luck. Why would my luck turn around now?

"Hey there." Zack eyes me up when we cross paths not far from Rodney's office. He was probably on his way in there to kiss the boss's butt or something. Or to complain about me. Or to kiss the boss's butt *while* complaining about me.

He eyes me up and down, a smile touching one corner of his mouth. His imminently kissable mouth. "Where are you heading?" he asks, checking his expensive watch. "Not quite time for lunch, is it?"

"I'm especially hungry today." I smile. "Somebody ruined my appetite last night, so I didn't get the chance to eat much at dinner."

"Hmm. Seems to me you were throwing down pretty hard on that large cheese pizza."

"You had the time to inspect the amount of pizza I ate while in the middle of that scene you created?"

He opens his mouth and it's so clear that he's ready to throw back a real zinger, but the appearance of a third party interrupts us.

"Hi, you two! My stars. What are you up to?" Rodney grins at us.

I clear my throat, willing myself to calm down. Why do we keep doing things like this in the middle of the office? Becca's words come back to me and I realize we're only adding fuel to the gossip garbage fire.

Zack manages to get the first word in, of course. "We're about to leave for a showing." He grins. "No big deal."

Why is he still alive? Why hasn't somebody killed him by now? I manage to keep my expression neutral, but it's a major effort.

He looks down at me, those icy eyes of his sparkling. "Isn't that right?"

"Right as always," I reply with a half-hearted smile.

He tilts his dark head. "You know, I was just about to ask you if we could take your car, rather than both of us driving separately."

Ooh, he's so stinking sneaky. And I'm so tired of feeling like we're playing a game of chess which only he's aware of. If we both go in my car, he can keep an eye on me.

Then again, I can keep an eye on him, too. Maybe this isn't such a bad idea.

"I love the way you two work together." Rodney smiles before walking away.

God, he's so painfully oblivious. I guess that works in our

favor, or else he'd know how badly things are going.

"I'll just get my coat," Zack says.

I could swear he's grinning as he turns away. I watch him striding down the hall to his cubicle. There's nothing for me to do but wait until he returns. We take the elevator in complete silence.

"Nice car," he murmurs as he slides into the passenger seat.

"Stop it."

"I'm serious. I was complimenting you. Can't a person compliment you?"

"It's nothing compared to your sex machine." I smirk.

"Oh, you don't know anything about my real sex machine."

At least I have an excuse to look over my left shoulder so my face is turned away from him so he can't see how red I have become. How is he so good at making me do that?

He taps his fingers on his thighs, clicking his tongue against his teeth in an obvious show of discomfort.

He's not alone in that.

"Sooo…" He looks around, searching for something to talk about. And the genius picks the worst possible thing, "Last night. Was that your sister you were having dinner with?"

Last night. When I would've shoved the rest of my pizza in his face if it hadn't been such a good pizza. "Yes. That's my sister. How did you know?"

"You look alike. Are you twins?"

"No. I'm older."

"Ah. Okay." More finger tapping. "It's nice, seeing sisters hanging out. So many siblings don't."

"I guess so."

"Do you guys get along well?"

I nod, focused on the road. "I'm her Maid of Honor, and we were having dinner as an excuse for her to obsess over details. Not that I mind. She's really stressed out over this."

"Weddings drive people nuts."

"That they do, evidently."

"You're a good sister," he offers.

It's so out of character, judging by the way we've been at each other's throats all this time, that I can't help feeling surprised. "How would you know that?"

"Because you humor her, instead of telling her where to get off with her obsessive wedding bullshit."

I can't help but laugh. "Oh, you have no idea how many times I've wanted to speak those very words."

"But you haven't."

"No. I haven't."

"Because you're a good sister." He sounds pleased with himself, having proven his point.

I'm about to tease him over a little when his phone rings.

That damn phone. Always interrupting things.

"Sorry," he mutters as he answers.

Immediately, I hear the sound of a woman's voice on the other end. A rather hysterical voice.

My hands clench the wheel until my knuckles go bone white.

Since we're already at the house by now, pulling into the roundabout, he gets out of the car at the first opportunity and continues his conversation.

Fabulous. I guess I'm on my own again.

But didn't I want to be?

So why is my blood boiling when I think of him on the phone with another woman? Would it be better if it were a client he was speaking to in secret? A client wouldn't sound that hysterical—at least, I'd hope not.

It doesn't matter, because he's off the phone well before the clients show up and things go well. By this time, we've both shown the house so many times it barely requires clear thought for me to rattle off the house's many advantages.

They leave, seeming happy but a little vague, and I can tell they won't make an offer. I think Zack got the same impression too. There's no way for him to rush off and leave me holding the bag, seeing as how we came in together so he hangs around and helps me tidy things up a bit.

As long as we don't both need to be in the library at the same time, we'll be fine. I don't know if I could face him in the room where we almost…

For some reason, the memory stirs me to anger. "So, it sounded like she was pretty upset," I snark over my shoulder as I polish the table in the entryway.

"What?" The sound of him beating a cushion comes to a halt.

"The girl on the phone earlier. She was upset. What'd you do? Barge into the restaurant where she was having dinner with her sister and cause a scene?" It's not nice. Nowhere close to it. But I can't help myself.

His sigh is heavy. Put-upon. "That was my sister. You have a sister with problems, so do I. Something in common. Crazy, huh?"

Yeah, right. A likely story. "What's her name?"

"Beth." He didn't have to think about it.

Well, so what? He has a sister named Beth. That doesn't mean it was her on the phone. "What was she upset about?"

Another sigh, though he keeps up the cushion rearranging. "She just had a bad break up. They were together for a long time. I used to think he was a decent guy, but my opinion has changed considerably." He sounds angry. Legitimately angry.

Is he that good an actor, or is he telling the truth? "What happened?" My voice is a little softer than before.

He shrugs. "Classic story. He was cheating on her. And now, just this morning, she found out he's with this girl. They're moving in together. Not even a full week after Beth and he broke up."

I wince. "Ouch. That's awful."

"I know. You have no idea how much I want to go over to this douchebag's new apartment and knock his head off." His beating has become quite... intense. Almost violent. The cushion is going to burst if he doesn't stop.

*He is telling the truth.*

"It's a shame we can't fight our loved ones' battles for them."

"Tell me about it. All we can do is be there for them when things go south." He glances my way with a crooked smile. "I'm about to say something which is going to sound ridiculous."

"Because that would be the first time you've ever said something ridiculous?"

He snorts, shaking his head. "Anyway, as I was about to say, it's a relief to be able to talk about it. Even if it's only you I'm talking to."

"Ha, ha, very funny." I smirk, rolling my eyes, but we both laugh.

Gee. Maybe he's somewhat human, after all. Maybe that night we had together wasn't only a way for him to get under my skin and trip me up.

Or maybe I'm letting my hormones get in the way again, like an idiot. I need to keep my head in the game, as the clock is ticking.

# SIENNA

We aren't back in the office for more than a few minutes before a new email comes through. I pull up closer to my laptop to make sure I'm reading it correctly.

The Dawsons want to see the house again. Today.

"Yes!" I whisper, pumping my arm in victory. Nobody can see me, so whatever. A second showing basically means they're ready to make an offer, and I know Nick is so desperate to unload the place at this point that he'll accept just about anything reasonable.

I have a good feeling about these people. I did from the first. They're not going to lowball me, and they're not just wasting my time. This is very good. A light at the end of the tunnel.

Zack's cc'd on the email, so I know he must see it, too. I manage to calm myself so as to not look like a complete doofus by running into his cubicle like a squealing schoolgirl.

Once I'm suitably serene, I walk over there like a normal

person. A mature person. One who's about to make a killing on a major sale.

"Hey." I grin, leaning in the doorway with my arms folded. "Did you see?"

But he doesn't look happy? Why not? He should look happy. Instead, he looks like somebody just killed his puppy.

"This is going to sound completely ridiculous, or maybe not, since I already explained the way things are with my little sis." He sits back in his chair, rubbing the bridge of his nose between two fingers. "I promised her I would see her today. Like, now-ish. I was just on my way out, and knowing the way things have been going, I'm fairly sure I won't be able to make it back to the office in time for the showing." He sounds pained and looks even worse. "This is why I was getting all those calls."

I can see the conflict he's going through, and I know how tough it can be. Then I realize how mad I was whenever he was on the phone during that showing and I feel bad. I've been there, too. So many times. Wanting to help Tami even when there are so many other things that need my attention.

Which is why I'm about to do something I would never do otherwise.

"You know what? Go ahead. I'll take care of things for both of us. And hey—if you can make it, that's great. You know how long second showings can take."

He blinks, hesitating like he's waiting for the punchline. "Are you serious?" he finally asks.

"Yes. Seriously. Beth needs you."

"No bullshit? No tricks?"

"Nope. I know what it's like to have a sister who needs your time. Don't sweat it. Seriously."

"All right." He smiles, still looking surprised. "You're doing me a huge favor. Thank you."

"I'm not doing it for you." I wink before backing away. "I'm doing it for your sister. Solidarity. Girl power. And all that."

And maybe a little bit for him. But only a little bit.

---

"Where's your boyfriend?" Mrs. Dawson asks when we meet in front of the house.

She would. He has that effect on women.

I ought to correct her. I really ought to. Shouldn't I? Yes. I should. But it would look childish and silly. So I don't. I've been accused of worse things than sleeping with Zack. "He had a family emergency," I say as I unlock the door. "I know he wanted to be here to see you again. I'm sorry."

"Not a problem," Mr. Dawson replies. "I'm just sorry to hear that."

Taking them through the house is a breeze, since they're so obviously in love with the place and each other. And they've been thinking a lot about what they'll do with it too. I overhear them murmuring about where they'll place the furniture and where they'll set up offices for themselves.

I can't believe it. This is looking better all the time.

I almost wish Zack was here for it. But no. It's better that he isn't.

"All right." They turn to me, after having one more whispered conversation on the other side of the kitchen. "I think we're ready to make a bid."

*Calm down, calm down, be professional. This is hardly the first time you've ever had a person make a bid before.*

I smile sweetly. "That's great news! I'm so glad. I was really hoping to be able to pair you two with this home. I can put the paperwork in today, if you wish."

"That would be fantastic." They're both beaming, so happy to be taking this big step.

Now, I can't help but feel the slightest bit of envy, truth be told. It must be nice, having a partner to celebrate these big life-altering moments with.

A moment that's not going to happen today, evidently.

"Shoot. I'm so sorry." My fingers fly over the files in my bag. "I didn't bring the paperwork with me." I was in too much of a rush and too off-balance because of dumb Zack and his dumb touching reaction to my offering to cover for him.

"Oh, no. That's disappointing, though, honestly, we never thought we'd get lucky enough to place the official bid today. But it would've been nice."

I can barely meet Mrs. Dawson's eyes. "I promise you, I'm not normally like this."

"We sprang this on you at the last minute," she says kindly. "I woke up this morning and thought, what are we waiting for? We know we want the house."

I hope she doesn't have the opposite realization tomorrow morning.

"How about we meet over lunch tomorrow, and I'll bring all the necessary paperwork with me then?" I suggest, mentally crossing my fingers that they won't think I'm too demanding.

To my relief, they agree, and we leave together. Though I'm smiling on the outside, on the inside I could kick myself. If it weren't for me being such an idiot, I could've maybe gotten the sale tied up today.

# SIENNA

*Just finished with Beth. Are you still there?*

I chew my lip and read the message again. I just pulled up to the office with every intention of making double sure the paperwork is ready in my bag tomorrow.

*Already at the office.*

My phone pings right back.

*How did it go?*

I smile as I type my reply.

*Went great. They want to make an offer. I also have a showing in the morning, which I wouldn't want to cancel since nothing's in writing yet. Lunch date tomorrow, though, to get the papers signed.*

Right away, I can see that he's typing up a reply.

*That's great news! Way to go.*

Darn him for making me feel all pleased with myself. Like his approval is what I'm interested in. Like I need that. It feels awkward, leaving things there. I should say something else for the sake of making conversation.

*How is your sister holding up?*

I hope that's not too personal a question—but then, he told me about her. It's not like her situation is a secret. I watch the cursor blink as he types his reply.

*Not great. She's learning more about this dude every day, even though I keep telling her not to bother. Just torturing herself.*

I know how the girl feels. That's the worst part. I don't know a single person who's ever had a bad breakup and hasn't wanted to stalk their ex a little. Especially if the ex was in the wrong.

*I'm sorry to hear that. Poor thing.*

My phone rings maybe half a second later.

"I hate sitting here, sending all these messages." He chuckles.

There's still an uneasiness between us, a newness. We straddle the line between civility and that weird tension between two people who made out on the floor in a house they're supposed to be selling.

"Yeah. I'm not the type to sit and exchange a million texts, either," I lie. I'd much rather talk via text than verbally.

Texting is pretty much my preferred means of communication outside work-related conversations.

"Listen. I was thinking. Maybe Beth needs to talk to a girl who's not one of her girlfriends. You know what I mean?"

"Sure. I can see that."

"So you'll do it?"

I close my eyes. "What?"

"I'm meeting her for dinner at the same restaurant you and I went to that first night. Remember?"

My heart races just a little faster. "Yes. I remember."

"It would be great if you could join us—it might help her to have an excuse to talk about something else. Someone else. Know what I mean?"

I know what he means. I know he's only doing this for his sister. It's obvious how much he cares for her, and I know what that feels like. I love my sister, too. "What time should I be there?"

Boy, I hope I don't end up regretting this.

# SIENNA

I t's always a shame to see bad things happen to nice girls.

Beth seems like a nice girl, for sure. Beautiful, too, though I don't know why that should be a surprise. She looks like a female version of Zack.

But fragile. And a little broken. She trusted her heart and her life to a man who betrayed her. I can tell she's trying to appear cheerful for her brother's sake, and possibly mine, but there's a deep well of sadness there.

"You're lucky to have a brother who cares so much about you." I can't help but look over at him, smiling to myself over the way he is smiling at her. Typical adoring big brother. I would never in a million years have imagined him behaving this way. "I've got to admit, I assumed he'd be the type who teased and tormented."

"Oh, he did plenty of that when we were kids." She laughs. "We beat each other up more times than I could count. Remember that one time you shoved me into the wall so hard, the sheetrock dented?" she asks, turning to him.

"What?" I gasp, laughing.

"In my defense, I'm fairly sure it was paper instead of sheetrock," he argues. "Those walls were painfully thin."

"Obviously!" Beth and I reply at the same time, giggling together.

"Scrawny little you?" she teases.

"He was scrawny?" I ask, eyeing him up and down in disbelief.

"You have no idea. Have you ever seen those old Popeye cartoons? What was her name? Olive Oyl!" Beth wipes tears of laughter away with the corner of her napkin.

I have to join her soon after because the thought of Zack being a scrawny, skinny little guy is just too delicious.

"Wow. One of you at a time is bad enough…" Zack says, shaking his head.

But I can tell he's enjoying seeing his sister lighten up a little, even if it's sort of at his expense. This goes on through our entrees and into dessert, which Beth and I decide to share.

Before long, it's time for me to go. "I have a few things to straighten out before a showing in the morning," I explain, giving Beth a hug before leaving.

"I'm so glad to have met you," she says, squeezing a little harder. "Zack never brings nice girls around."

"Hey…" he warns, shaking his head.

"I know, I know, you two work together." She shrugs. "But still. That doesn't mean she isn't nice."

"She has a good point." I grin while sliding into my coat.

He walks me to the car, leaving his sister sipping her cappuccino.

When we're alone in the parking lot, he asks, "Okay. Why did you really come here tonight?"

"For starters, I like the food." I glance at him from the corner of my eye and see he's not smiling.

"But I thought you hated me?" he says softly.

His question reminds me of when I accused him of the same thing. He's so good at doing that. The memory of an elephant, and the poor manners to bring up what he remembers.

When we finally reach my car, I'm glad for it. He's making me uncomfortable, but not in a terrible sort of way. In the sort of way that brings a flush to my cheeks and makes the back of my neck tingle.

"All right. The truth." I lean with my back to the car, and look up at him. Oh, my God, bad idea. The tingles go right down my spine. "I feel sorry for Beth. I know what it is like, being with a man I thought was mine, only to find out how wrong I was when he belonged to someone else. I think almost everyone in the world past puberty knows that feeling."

"True," he murmurs with a rueful smirk.

"My heart feels for her. It truly does. And, honestly?" I look into his eyes, straight into them, locking and holding on without blinking. "And for you, too."

"For me?" His eyebrows rise a little as he points to himself.

"Yes. Because you're only trying to do your best for her. You want to take away her pain, maybe inflict a little damage on the jerk who's done this to her."

"A little?"

I smile, hearing that big brother growl of his. He wants to hurt this guy, maybe tear his throat out. Or tear off a part of his body he might miss even more. I'd want to do the same to Luke if he ever did something like this to Tami. "I guess I just know how difficult it is to be another person's support system, especially when they're going through a really hard time."

"What about your parents?" he asks.

An unconscious sigh escapes me. "My Dad died of cancer when we were quite young. When we were teenagers my mom married a man who doesn't like to share her with anyone. Don't get me wrong, he's very good to her, just madly possessive, you know." I wrinkle my nose. "To make her life easier my sister and I don't call her unless she calls us."

For some strange reason, we've both become completely serious now. The air around us changes. I clear my throat and carry on, "Being the older one, I promised Dad I'd take care of Tami, so that's what I do. It can be pretty exhausting at times, but she family and I love her." I'm sure I'm babbling now, but I can't stop. If I stop, something else is going to happen. "The fact that you're hanging in and doing your best for her means you must be tired."

He stares at me, but he's no longer listening to me.

Tell me how crazy I am, but our bodies are now doing the

talking. I feel my body leaning towards him. Then a family exits the restaurant, their children race into the carpark shouting and the spell is broken

"I'll never let her down," he says softly.

I smile up at him, admiring the way the moonlight makes his eyes glitter like a precious jewel and the way they shine warmly down on me. "I didn't think you would." My voice is just a whisper. Then I turn away and start fumbling with my car door.

## ZACK

I expected Beth to ask a bunch of questions about Sienna once we were alone.

I didn't expect what she puts me through the second I return to my seat.

"Sooo…" She swirls what's left of the cappuccino in her cup. "What's the story with you and my new bestie?"

"You like her because she helps you make fun of me."

"You are such a baby!"

"Hardly. But two against one is hardly fair." I love seeing her like this, with mischief in her eyes. She's her old self. She can forget about her problems for a little while, and I'm more than happy to play along if it means she keeps her good mood.

"Oh, get over it. Such a big shot, and you can't stand a little teasing. You can give as good as you get, and I know it, so don't try to play victim with me."

She's right about that. Haven't I sparred with Sienna more than once? I like it. Probably more than a little too much.

"Anyway," she continues after finishing her drink, "You know what I'm asking, so don't try to act like you don't. Who is she, really?"

"She's really the woman I'm working with to sell a house, like I told you. She's someone from the office."

"Riiiiight." She rolls her eyes and shakes her head mournfully.

"What is that supposed to mean?"

"It's supposed to mean that the two of you were making goo-goo eyes at each other the entire time she was here."

"What? Was this before or after you verbally eviscerated me?"

"My, my, such vocabulary." Another eye roll, just like I remember. "Before and after, for your information."

"In that case, you'll be very surprised to hear that she doesn't even like me very much. In fact, we don't get along well at all."

"Hmm. Since when are you in the habit of inviting women you don't get along with to dinner?"

I look around, spreading my arms in a shrug. "You act like you weren't here with us! Like this was a date."

"I might as well have not been for half the time, with you guys staring at each other like you were trying to figure out how to most quickly get into each other's pants. I mean, I felt a little embarrassed."

"Knock it off."

"Hey." She holds up her hands, palms out. "You can keep lying to yourself if you want. Whatever helps you sleep at night."

"You're very imaginative."

"And you're very dense if you think I can't see through you. Nobody's known you longer than me, except for our parents. So just save your stories, okay?"

"You should see some of the fights we've gotten into, and the shitty things we've done to each other over this house we're working on together."

She frowns. "Why?"

I sigh. It sounds so stupid when I say it out loud, "Both of us wanted to take the sale for ourselves, rather than sharing, but it was mostly my fault. She was willing to share at the beginning."

"You and I did some shitty things to each other when we were kids," she points out, tilting her head to the side. "And we didn't hate each other. I mean… okay, we hated each other, but not really."

"I get what you're saying. Just trust me. It's not that way for us. Okay?"

"Fine, fine."

"And we're about ready to accept a bid on the place, anyway, so there's that. It's practically sold, so we'll never have to work together again," I add.

"Oh, well, good! You won't be working together anymore." She grins like the Cheshire cat, the smug thing. "That's a good thing. Right?"

I feel empty inside when she says it that way. "Yeah. That's a good thing." I signal for the check.

# SIENNA

"You ready for this?" Zack's smile is genuine as he enters my cubicle the next morning, after my return from what I hope is the last showing of Nick's house.

I have to admit, something about having dinner with him and his sister has softened my opinion of him quite a bit. I would ordinarily feel a little miffed at him walking right into my private space like this without so much as a knock, but now I feel that it's just not worth getting worked up over. In fact, I kinda like it that we have this new bond.

God, who am I becoming?

"Of course. I eat lunch meetings for… breakfast."

He smiles at my lame attempt at humor. "Seriously, they're a great couple."

"Yeah, I got a good feeling about them right off. Even if they think we're a couple, too."

"Well, we almost were one a couple of days back."

I wish my heart didn't flutter when he said that. It's getting harder to resist his charm, the charm I used to hate, the charm that made me gag whenever I heard him shower other women with it. I open my mouth, think better, and close it again.

His smile widens, dimples showing in his cheeks.

Crap. What were we talking about again? *Right. The lunch meeting.* "So about lunch…"

"Do you want to take point on this, since you're the one who was with them yesterday?" he asks.

Wow. It takes a second for me to get over my surprise. "You're sure about that? It isn't like you to just step aside and let someone else take the lead."

"No…it's fine. There are no egos here."

Is it wrong that I burst out laughing? I tell myself it probably is, but I can't help it. "Since when?"

Anything he has to say in return is lost when my phone rings. "My sister," I murmur, sort of relieved for the interruption. He makes a move to leave, but I motion for him to stay as I answer.

"Oh, my God!" she sobs before launching into a story I can't understand thanks to the way she won't stop crying.

"Tami. Tami? Tami!" I glance at Zack, who puts his hands up and starts backing away, but I gesture with my hand that he should stay. "Honey, I need you to calm down and start again. I couldn't understand a word of what you just said."

She takes a deep, shaky breath, then blows it out. "The florist.

They just called and said they overbooked and won't be able to handle me."

"Oh, no." I rub my temples, eyes closed.

"What am I supposed to do? With no flowers? They were supposed to be so professional!" She's ramping up again, ready to go full-on meltdown.

I need to calm her and quickly. "Sweetheart, we can make this right."

"You're the one who wanted them!"

"I know. I feel terrible about it. But I'm certain we'll find something. Just… let me think about it for a minute, okay?"

"We don't have a minute," she almost shouts.

I hold the phone away from my ear. "Yes, we do. I know you think this is unfixable, but it isn't. We'll figure something out." Only I don't know what. And I really don't have time to devote to this at the moment, seeing as how I have the biggest closing of my career within my grasp.

"I don't see how." She breaks down again, crying into the phone.

I look up at Zack, unsure of what to do.

*"Go to her,"* he mouths, nodding.

I raise my eyebrows. He can't be serious. Although, I did cover for him yesterday.

"I mean it," he whispers. "Go. It's all right."

I don't know that I feel entirely comfortable with this, but I feel even worse knowing my sister will spend the rest of the day in hysterics if I don't do something to help and fast. "Where are you?" I ask her.

"In my car, outside work. I didn't want anybody to see me like this."

Good thing, too. At least she had the sense to leave the office. "Okay. I'll meet you there. We'll figure something out, I promise."

"You'll come? Now?"

One more look at Zack before replying, "Yes. I'll come now. Just stay there." When I hang up, I let out a heavy sigh and slump in my chair.

"That sounded pretty terrible," Zack observes, his voice softened with sympathy.

"I feel awful about it. I was the one who pushed for this florist. They seemed so great and I heard nothing but good things. Their work is beautiful. Now, I'm the heel who recommended them."

"It happens. Plans fall through. This isn't your fault. I'll handle the Dawsons while you go to her and figure out the solution."

I can't help but eye him suspiciously. We've only been at this friendly stage for around a minute or so, and I'm not entirely sure that he can be trusted. "If I didn't know better, I'd think this was a ploy for you to seal the deal on your own and get all the credit."

It's like I flipped a switch and the lights went out. One second, he's warm and caring. The next, his face goes cold. "Are we still on that? You honestly still think I'm that low?"

"Don't take it so seriously." I shouldn't have said it. I should've kept it to myself. All the progress we've made just disappeared, and all because I was too stupid to keep my mouth shut.

"No. I will take it seriously, because I thought we were better than that now." He turns away, shaking his head. "Maybe I'm not the black-hearted creep you think I am."

I feel around two inches tall and wish we were anywhere but in the office. I could stop him, ask for his forgiveness, try to talk it out. In front of our coworkers? Impossible.

All I can do is get my things together and head over to where my sister is waiting for me. I hope I'm more of a comfort to her than I was a partner to Zack just now.

I need a win today.

# ZACK

I can't believe her. No way, she's real. Real people aren't so damn suspicious. Always on the lookout in case, somebody takes advantage of them. All right, sure, I started things off this way, but how many more hoops do I have to jump through to get her to chill out? And stop seeing me as an opponent.

Hell, I even encouraged her to go help her sister, when I could've insisted the Dawsons like her and she had to come to lunch with me to make sure we got the bid taken care of. Something niggles at the back of my mind. The truth is maybe she can't trust me because her intuition is picking up some subtle signs from me. I haven't been totally honest with her.

No wonder she suspects something is up, even if she doesn't know what it is.

I push all of it out of my head as I enter the restaurant. It is one of those upscale casual places that tries to be a lot better than it is. Hipster-preppy. Not normally my taste, but the customer is always right.

Everything is riding on this. More than ever.

"Zack!" The Dawsons walk in just behind me.

Mrs. Dawson looks around, smiling. "Where's Sienna? It seems like we can never get the two of you together at the same time anymore."

I force a smile. "She had an emergency to attend to, came up just a little while ago. She was very sorry to miss this."

"What a shame," she replies, tsking. "Never mind, I'm sure we can get everything squared away."

"Certainly. I have the paperwork with me. And I'm sure she'll do what she can to hurry, too. She did want to sit down with you."

But something tells me she won't be able to make it in time.

Damn it. I hate that I missed the lunch.

But at least I solved the florist issue. A phone call to them, a few references to the contract and deposit my sister put down and a polite, yet firm, demand that they put me in touch with another florist willing to take on the work. To honor the deposit already paid or a legal letter would be on their desk Monday morning and suddenly... we were back on track.

They were magically able to clear the space in their schedule.

And I get it. I do. They're busy, highly in demand, fantastic at what they do. It isn't easy to turn down the prospect of new work, probably bigger than my sister's wedding. At the end of the day, they're a small business with the ever-present need to build their client base.

However, they also made a promise to my sister, and I'll be damned if I let them walk all over her.

All is great again in her world as I stroll into the office, well past the point where hauling ass to the restaurant would make any sense. It's already past two o'clock. I'm a little disappointed, honestly, that Tami didn't have the presence of mind to hold them to account and I had to drop the most important deal of my career to sort her out.

I hate feeling like I let anyone down. And I have let Zack down. The Dawsons had gotten comfortable with me and they were expecting me. But I helped Tami. And I'll remember that when I carry my bouquet on the day of her wedding. If Dad were alive, he would've been proud of me today. He always said, *"You're in charge. Take care of your sister now."*

The sounds of typing coming from Zack's office tell me he's back. I have a decision to make: slip past his cubicle without a word because I feel like an idiot for what I said earlier, or face him like a grown, professional woman.

Darn it. I hate being a grownup sometimes.

"Hi." I step just inside the doorway, lingering in case he decides to tell me to get lost.

He hesitates before turning around in his chair. "Oh. Hi." He's blank faced.

"How'd it go?"

"How do you think?"

I sure do wish he'd be a little more... something. Angry, happy, whatever. So long as he'd show a little feeling instead of looking and sounding so flat. "You... got the paperwork signed?"

Another hesitation. Doesn't he know he's driving me to the brink of insanity here? I want to crawl out of my skin, I'm so agitated. "Okay. I guess I'll go, then," I whisper, unnerved and disappointed.

"Come on." He grins suddenly, the biggest, brightest grin I have ever seen anybody undertake. "Of course, everything went fine. It's all in order—in fact, I just shot a message off to Nick to let him know we're ready to move forward, that we'll need his signature and all that. It should only take another couple of days at this point, depending on his availability."

I clutch my chest and start laughing with relief. He had me worried for a minute there, and he knew it. He likes knowing he threw me off, too. I can tell by the way one corner of his mouth quirks up in a smile… all at once sexy and infuriating.

I guess I deserve it a little, after insulting him earlier.

"Now that we have that out of the way, we should celebrate." He folds his hands in front of himself, elbows on the arms of his chair. "Dinner's on me."

"Another dinner?" I purse my lips, pretending to think it over. "Hmm. So long, as it's not Italian. I've had enough of that lately."

He chuckles. "Done." As I'm leaving, a smile on my face, he adds, "Did everything go all right with your sister? Sorry, I should've asked before now."

"Everything's great. Nothing a well-worded warning about the power of a signed contract couldn't fix."

"Atta girl." He grins. "I knew you'd set things right."

For a moment there, he sounds like the sort of supportive man I've always wanted in my life. It's a shame he's not actually *in* my life.

# SIENNA

"Tell me something." I lean forward, conspiratorial. "Did you really almost put your sister through a wall?"

Is it my imagination, or is he blushing ever so slightly?

Zack shrugs. "She makes it sound a lot worse than it is. And all these years later, there's little way for me to defend myself."

"That's not an answer," I remind him, my voice light and somewhat teasing. My skin feels warm and my stomach is all fluttery. Who I am turning into?

"All right. The truth. She was a bruiser," he replies, shrugging. "No man likes to admit that his sister - his younger sister, at that - beat his ass when they were kids, but there you are. She played field hockey, for God's sake."

I can't help but laugh. "I guess it helped inspire you to build your body up a little, huh?" If that's the case, Beth did the world a favor.

"It was part of the reason," he admits with a chuckle. "And you're the only person in the world who knows this, so keep it confidential."

"Your secret's safe with me." I wink.

"I guess there comes a time in everybody's life when their sister or brother drives them to that point when you lose it and just want to kill them." He grins.

"Oh, yes. Tami and I used to throw down, I'm not happy to admit."

"Usually, I'd give her a shove and that would be her excuse to put me in a headlock or something similarly humiliating," he admits, rubbing the back of his neck. He's cheeks are flushed.

It's rather endearing, knowing Mr. Perfect wasn't always so perfect.

"Until that day when it all got to be too much," I say.

"Yeah. I shoved just the right way, she hit a cheaply made archway, and the rest, as they say, is history." He smiled with the memory. "You can imagine how horrified our parents were at the damage. I was grounded for a month."

"To younger sisters." I raise my wine glass in a toast, which he mimics with a rueful chuckle.

I hate to admit it, but I'm liking him more and more all the time. Now that there's no more rivalry between us, no more childishness, I can relax and enjoy him for the person he is.

I like the person he is.

I like him a lot.

And if I'm not mistaken, I think he likes me, too. Now that

there's no ulterior motive for him to flirt with me it's a lot easier to believe he's not putting on an act. He really is this warm, this personable. This freaking charming.

Ugh. Why does he have to be so charming? Isn't it enough that he's gorgeous and sexy?

You use to hate that charm, a voice in my head reminds me. Yes, I did, but that was when I saw him as a rival. We don't have to be rivals anymore, or enemies. There's more than enough room for both of us, more than enough sales to make.

There's a good chance I've had too much wine.

"Sienna!" I recognize Mark's voice before I feel the touch of his hand on my shoulder. "What a surprise, seeing you here."

It's an effort, plastering on a smile when I look up at him. He would have to come by at the worst possible time, wouldn't he? Poor timing was always one of his undesirable qualities. And there were many to choose from.

"How are you?" I ask, not really wanting to know. But in a situation like this, one has to observe the niceties.

"Just great. You know, I was thinking about reaching out to arrange another showing of that house." He hasn't stopped touching my shoulder since he approached, and he has deliberately avoided acknowledging Zack's presence.

"Really?" I ask, still smiling through clenched teeth. "I'm sorry, but it looks as though it's been sold."

His pleased expression falters just a little.

I enjoy this very much since I know he has no real interest in the house. Just a ploy to make me run after him.

"Yes," Zack adds, his voice somewhat louder than it strictly needs to be. "We came out to celebrate her success with the sale."

God bless him.

Mark shoots a look his way, finally forced into acknowledging the fact that I'm not alone.

As far as I'm concerned, Zack couldn't have chosen his words better. The one thing Mark would never do when we were together was celebrate my victories.

Boy. I'm liking him more and more every minute.

The best part, the very best part, is the way Zack stares at Mark. His eyes are narrowed in a challenging way, and his mouth curls in something between a smirk and a sneer.

Oh, my God. He's jealous. He's actually jealous. Can it be? Mr. Wonderful, Mr. Sexy, Mr. Every Woman's Fantasy, is jealous? Over me? It makes me want to stand up and do a happy dance right there in the middle of that crowded restaurant.

"I see." Mark's hand drops from my shoulder so fast it was as if I had suddenly burst into flames. "Congratulations."

"Thanks." I wait until he has walked away before my eyes shift back to Zack. "And thanks."

"A bit of an overstatement, wouldn't you say? Telling him the house is sold?"

I notice how uncomfortable he looks now, like an unsettled animal. Mark has riled him. "Whatever." I shrug, finishing off my wine. "He's not interested in the house. Not really. I hardly think I lost us a sale."

"I wouldn't let him buy it, anyway." His voice is close to a growl.

"Why not?"

"Because I don't like the looks of him." He stands rather abruptly, surprising me. "You know what? I'd love a nightcap, but not here. Somewhere a little quieter, where we won't be so easily interrupted."

I look up at him and notice the way he looks down at me. The possessive look in his eye. The way the muscles of his shoulders and arms work beneath his shirt as he slides into his coat.

Yes. Yes, I would like an intimate nightcap very much.

# SIENNA

He's a real contradiction, this Zack. Just when I think I have him figured out, he throws me a curve ball.

Judging from the sort of car he drives and, of course, the expensive clothing and watches, I was sure his house would be a showplace. The sort of house that would put a modest little saltbox like mine to shame.

Nothing could be further from the truth. In fact, our houses could've been built off the same plans.

"This is where you live?" I ask as I climb from my car, parked beside his in a short, wide driveway.

"What's wrong with it?" he asks.

"You're reading me wrong, as always. I expected your house to be more… like your car, I guess."

He laughs. "There's only me here and I like someplace homey. Comfortable. You know?"

"Sure. I'm the same way," I admit.

"You don't know how many ridiculous apartments and houses I've been inside; cold, immaculate places only one person lives in but could fit twenty."

"Oh, you mean the house we're currently trying to sell?" I laugh as we step inside the living room, just off the front door.

"Something like that." He flips on the light, revealing a living room with a beautiful fireplace set in a brick wall, an over-stuffed sofa, an entire wall covered in shelves nearly over-flowing with books.

Who is this man?

"Can I fix you something to drink?" he asks, walking to the kitchen.

I follow close behind, admiring the small office to one side and the dining room to the other before stepping into a thor-oughly modern, thoroughly lived-in kitchen.

"Honestly? I think I should stick to water if I'm driving," I admit. My head's spinning a bit, but that could be from the company and the overwhelming feeling that I have no idea who I'm truly dealing with.

He pulls a bottle from a refrigerator stocked with a mixture of fresh food and takeout containers. All right, so that's not entirely outside my opinion of him. But the cast iron skillet on the stove catches my attention, and I have to ask about it.

He beats me to it. "I was frying chicken a few nights back," he explains.

"You fry chicken?"

"It's one of my favorite meals. Granted, I have to put in a few extra laps at the pool every time I make it, but I'm not complaining."

I perch on a stool around the island in the center of the room. "What else do you cook?"

"Play your cards right and you'll find out for yourself one day." He grins, leaning his elbows on the island.

I lean over, too, meeting him in the middle. I can't help it. He's too charming, too charismatic. A magnet. The opposite of me in many ways, but isn't that when magnets attract each other?

I have to stop myself from climbing over the island and taking the front of his shirt in my hands when our mouths meet and it feels like the world is finally right. Why have I passed a single day of my life without kissing this delicious man? Our mouths were made for each other, fitting together perfectly as they move together.

In my fantasy, other things fit perfectly too…

Things happen and I find myself lying on my stomach on the cool granite of the island surface. With a tug, he slides me over to him. He lifts me bodily. Oh my, this man is really strong. He made that look effortless. Sitting me on the surface, he stands between my thighs. I pull him in, wrapping my legs around his waist and holding tight. All that matters in the world right now is being close to him.

His hands slide over my back before finding the zipper of my dress and sliding it down to my waist. I slide out, letting it fall to my hips, throwing my head back as his mouth skims my throat, and over my chest.

I gasp when his tongue slides between my breasts, lighting

me on fire, sending shockwaves straight to my core. My skin tingles for more, every nerve on fire. I need more—all of him. It's a relief when he unclasps my bra and closes his lips around one nipple. My back arches, my body offering itself to him in a desperate plea.

He works the dress down, over my legs, to the floor, before easing me down onto my back and letting his mouth explore me.

I close my eyes, fingers tangled in his hair, guiding him and letting him take control of me all at once. "Zack... Zack..." I whisper, my head rolling back and forth, losing myself. God, so much pleasure. Sensation rolls over me in waves as his tongue laps at my increasingly sensitive skin. My stomach, my navel, the hem of my panties while he slowly, inch, by torturous inch, slides them down.

"So good..." he growls, kissing the insides of my thighs.

My hips jerk upward on their own, meeting his mouth.

Looking up into my eyes, he slides his tongue between my slit.

My clit pulses. "Oh Jesus," I gasp as he runs it along the length of my cleft before sucking my whole pussy into his mouth.

I scream, completely lost now. It's been so long and he's oh, so good. He eats me as if he's been starving for a taste of me. He's not doing it as if it's a favor to me, as if he wants to get on with other things. He does it as if there is nothing else in the world he'd rather be doing. As if he's lost in the flavor of me. There's something so hot about a man who is enjoys pleasuring a woman that much.

This man just loves driving me crazy, making me writhe and gasp, making me grind my pussy against his face because I'm an animal. He's turning me into an animal. And I love it. I can let out everything I've been holding back.

He wants me to. His hands find mine, our fingers lacing together as he continues to work my clit with his skillful tongue. We're in this together. And somehow, this is what pushes me over the edge. My back arches as I come, letting loose a torrent of screams that seem to shake the kitchen.

It's a revelation. Like being born again. Tears threaten to spill over onto my cheeks as I sit up, holding him close while my body continues to shake from the force of my orgasm.

This is what I've been missing? Not just sex, but connection? Now I know why it always felt like something was off, just slightly wrong. Because this is so much more than physical. I don't know what to do with what I'm going through.

He just holds me. No words. He lets me feel what I'm feeling. Even though his dick is hard, pressing against me. Even though he's breathing heavily, almost grunting with desire. He holds me while strange tears fill my eyes and roll down my face. He doesn't let go until I've calmed completely down, and show him I'm ready for more by letting my hand slip down the cords of tight muscles in his stomach.

I unbutton and unzip his pants to show him how much more I'm ready for, then unbutton his shirt while he takes care of unrolling a condom over his thick, straining length. God, he's so big. Even bigger than what he was in my fantasy. Of course, he is. He's perfection.

Taking my butt in his hands, he pulls me to the edge of the

counter in one quick jerk before sliding into my waiting folds.

I can't help but gasp sharply as he parts me and sinks in deep. "Oh, my God, Zack," I whisper against the side of his neck while he takes me, thrusting smoothly. All I can do is hold on, my arms around his shoulders, my legs around his hips as he rides me, driving us both to the point of grunting and panting as we take what we need from each other.

While we make something else.

I move back and our eyes meet. I hold his gaze as he begins to lose control of his pace and his rhythm. I'm losing it again, too, my muscles tightening around him—which only drives him even crazier, his breath hot on my skin as the muscles of his throat strain at the increased pressure.

"Yes… yes, Zack, please…" I don't know what I'm asking for.

He doesn't seem to mind. He crushes my body to his before pummeling me with a furious burst of sharp, deep thrusts and I let go, leaning against him as my body shudders in release.

His roar fills the air around us as he comes with me, and we stay that way. Locked together until we catch our breath.

When he pulls away, I expect a little nervous laughter, a little apology, or the inevitable questions of whether everything is okay or worse… was it as good for me as it was for him.

What I don't expect is his growl as he lifts me into his arms like a caveman and carries me away from the kitchen. "I haven't shown you the bedroom yet."

As soon as I lay her on the bed, my hands lock on her ankles. Pulling them wide apart I stare down at her pussy. Pink, wet, and quivering with excitement. My gaze rises up to her face.

Sienna looks up at me, her eyes wide.

"That's one pretty cunt you have there, babe."

She blushes, the color seeping into her cheeks, and I let my eyes roam over her glorious nakedness. Part of me can't believe she's on *my* bed, buck naked, her legs wide open for *me*. For so long, she was the hot bitch at the office who looked at me as if I was dirt at the bottom of her shoes. Who'd have thought I'd be eating her pussy.

Without warning, I flip her onto her stomach. She gasps as I spread her legs and tilt her hips upwards so her pussy and fine ass are opened up and completely exposed to me. Beautiful. Just beautiful.

"Keep that position," I order.

As my face gets closer, her scent invades my senses, making it hard for me to even think straight. I don't tease, or mess around this time. I go straight for her clit, sucking the engorged, sensitive nub into my mouth.

Her hips jerk with surprise at the sudden assault, but I grasp her outer thighs and holding firm, run my tongue along her slit. She tastes like heaven. It drives me so wild I swear I could fucking come just from eating pussy. With great dedication, I give myself over to the task of feasting on her sweet flesh.

"Oh, Zack… Oh, Zack," she chants again and again, as if her brain is so scrambled she can't find any other words.

As I devour her, my fingers get busy fucking her hard. When she is nearly over the edge, I pull my fingers out of her, flip myself onto my back and order, "Straddle my face, Honey. I want you to come on my face."

She obeys quickly, her ripe breasts bouncing. I watch as she raises her lush bottom into the air and hovers, her glistening folds inches over my face. I have to admire its beauty, the splayed crevice between her cheeks, and the little puckered orifice. As I watch, that little hole move up over my nose towards my eyes, and her dripping slit lowers over my mouth.

My tongue extends before she is even within reach. A drop of her nectar leaks onto my tongue. Taking one last look at her cute anal orifice, I raise my head and push my tongue into her giddy sweetness. She shudders at the tongue fucking.

My five o'clock shadow rasps against her soft skin. There's going to be marks left behind, but right now, she doesn't even register the burn. Throwing her head back, she rides my face hard until she finds her release in a great rush, her thighs squeezing my head. Her cum floods out of her into my mouth and face as I lick it eagerly.

For a few seconds afterwards, Sienna doesn't move as she enjoys the aftermath of euphoria and the sweet sensation of my tongue meandering all over her pussy. Then she turns her body sideways and looks down at me. "I fucking love this position," she exclaims, a wicked glint in her eyes.

"I bet you do," I reply between licks.

"Haven't you had enough?" she asks a cheeky look in her eyes.

I spear her swollen flesh with my tongue. "I'm never going to get enough of this."

"Did I ever tell you I love to suck cock?" she asks, her teeth snagging her reddened, swollen bottom lip.

Fancy that, she's shy. It's so fucking sexy.

"A girl who likes to suck cock. Where have you been all my life?" I tease.

She shrugs. "I know. It's weird, but I just love the feeling of having a cock in my mouth, the way it throbs on my tongue, the silkiness of it."

I raise my eyebrows in surprise.

"Not to brag or anything, but I'm almost porn-star good at giving a blowjob," she pauses and looks at me wickedly. "But I've never, never had such a gloriously huge cock like yours. I don't know if I will be able to deep throat something that big, but I'm planning on giving it a damn good try."

I chuckle.

"To be honest," she adds, "I actually can't wait to taste you. You've got the kind of cock I'd like to gently nurse for as long as possible."

"In that case, let's begin. We have all night my eager little cock sucker."

Instantly, she lays forward on top of me.

The sensuous move gives me an irresistible view of her pink bits. I snarl and bite one of her ass cheeks.

She moans and licks my erect cock like it is a lollipop. "God, you taste so good," she purrs.

Knowing fully well she is driving me insane she plays with my dick mercilessly, stroking it with maddening slowness, tracing each vein from base to tip with the tip of her tongue. With each torturous action, she turns around and looks arrogantly into my eyes, knowing she has me exactly where she wants me. Right now, she's the one with all the power.

She sucks the entire head into her hot mouth, and I groan.

It's a shame I can't enjoy watching my dick disappear into her pretty face. As she sucks, she takes more and more in with each bob of her head. Fuck, I'm so horny I have to stop myself from blowing my load.

To level the field, I pull up my head and feast once more on Sienna's hot, sticky flesh. She squirms, but I get my hands up between us and use my fingers to spread her lips so I can get deeper into those slick folds. I lick every inch of her as she moans, screams, wriggles and grinds her sex against my face in blissful pleasure.

Suddenly, her ass cheeks clench my face tighter, and she climaxes with a forceful blast of warm liquid. At that moment, I stop trying to hold and let myself come too, spurting into her mouth while she sucks hard and milks every last drop out of me. When it is over, she slumps on top of me, drained and exhausted.

"Yeah, you take a little rest, sweetheart, because I'm not finished with you yet."

# SIENNA

O h. My. God.

The first thing that goes through my head on opening my eyes is utter horror. Just a rush of complete horror at myself.

What was I thinking? Why did I do this?

I've never done anything like it in my life. Sleeping with a colleague. As if I needed to further complicate things.

Sure, it seemed like a good idea at the time. It seemed like an extremely good idea. One of those ideas a person goes through with even when their intellect tells them it's prob-ably the worst thing they could possibly do. Because in certain situations—hormones are more powerful than good sense.

Which is an awful shame.

Not that it wasn't fun. It was mind-blowingly fun, the sort of fun I haven't had in way too long. Not that it wasn't more than fun. No matter what happens, I'll never forget the sense of connection with him last night. I'll never forget the rush of emotion, and the way he allowed me to work my way through that. And not that there is a huge part of me that's just loving the fact that I'm waking up in his bed.

It's just that things sure would be better if I didn't have to see him at work today. Yes. That would be better.

His deep, even breathing is just behind me. Thank God, he doesn't have an arm draped over me or something. I'm not much of a sleep cuddler. I need my space. Maybe's he's the same way.

I would love to explore the other ways in which we're compatible, because, judging by last night, we are certainly compatible, very compatible. But getting out of here is much more important right now. While he's sleeping. It'll be hard enough to face him in the office.

I hear stirring coming from the bedroom as I slip out the front door.

Whew. Just made it.

---

I 'm not so lucky on arriving at work, however. In fact, it looks as though he's waiting for me at the elevator. What are the odds that we just happen to arrive at the same time?

His phone is in one hand and he's scrolling through messages on it and the other is grasping a cup of coffee. Looking like sex on two legs, especially now that I know what he looks like during orgasm.

My heart races a little as I approach. "Good morning," I

murmur, keeping my eyes on the floor. Oh, God, what's he thinking? Is he going to be cool? I remind myself he's an adult, as am I, and I'm certain a man like him has been through more than his share of one-night stands over the course of his life.

He clears his throat like he might want to say something, but he's interrupted by a member of the accounting department whose name I don't know.

Penny? Patty?

Whoever she is, she's young and cute and she seems to know him. "Good morning," she greets giddily, batting her eyelashes.

I wonder how she'd feel if I tore them all out.

He barely looks up in acknowledgement, only glancing away from his phone for a split second.

*Ha! Take that*, I say to myself, glaring at the back of her head as we step onto the elevator.

The door swishes shut and I concentrate my attention on the lighted panel above the doors. At least there's an excuse for us to stay silent. It's not like we could discuss last night in front of this girl, whatever her name is. Though, I'd love to see her reaction.

I'd love to see everyone's reaction, honestly. After all, I hated him a week ago and everyone knew it. And everyone loved watching the sparks fly between us. I wonder if any bets were laid, and if anyone had us sleeping together at this point.

I guess they saw what I didn't want to see. I should talk to him. Shouldn't I? I ought to at least thank him for dinner, as ridiculous as that would be. We'd both know what I was really referring to, but it might at least be a decent segue into discussing how we'll handle being in the office together.

To my eternal relief, I get an email as we're stepping off the elevator. Great, I have an excuse to speak to Zack.

Penny/Polly/whatever her name is walks on ahead.

"Do you see this?" I asked, pointing to my phone. "Kent. Now he wants to make an offer."

He checks his phone, an eyebrow quirking up. "I don't have a message. Seems you're the only one who got the email." His smile is tight, knowing. Kent only wants an excuse to meet up with me, and we both know it.

"It's a shame he's missed his opportunity," I reply, meaning much more than my words imply on the surface. And I think he knows it, because he smiles slowly.

My breath catches and I stare into his eyes as if I'm hypnotized.

One of our colleagues passes by. "How's it hanging?" he calls.

Zack frowns. "Catch you later," he says softly to me.

I nod. This thing is stronger than me. I'm not going to try and resist it. Why should I? It feels so damn good.

He is smiling as he heads to his cubicle.

I head to mine, determined to let Kent know there's no chance of anything happening. As for getting any further work done, I have no clue how it'll be possible. I can't keep my brain focused on one thing at a time for more than a few seconds, since I can't stop wondering whether he'll tell everyone about what happened.

No, that's not his style. He's many things, but I doubt he maintains that frat boy mentality. Comparing notes on the girls they've slept with. He's not like that.

Isn't he? What do I really know about him? My mind starts obsessing about him, us, me. A half hour passes, feeling like a million years. I'm stunned when I check the time. It's not even lunch yet, that's how out of it I am. I haven't accomplished a thing yet. What is going on with me? I haven't even written up my to-do list, the way I do every single morning.

Maybe I'll ask him to lunch. I mean, he bought dinner last night. It's only fair I take him out for a meal next. Yes, that's what I'll do. I'll take him to lunch. I manage to get up the courage to go to his cubicle, my legs shaking all the way, and he's not even at his desk.

The desk isn't empty, though. I move closer to it. My heart is beating fast. There's a contract sitting on it. A contract with the signatures of the Dawsons on it.

*And only Zack's name as the seller.*

"No," I whisper, going to it, flipping through. There must be a mistake. There has to be. He wouldn't cheat me like that not after…

Not after, he got me into bed. Not after, he seduced me by taking me to dinner, by bringing me into his life and humanizing himself to me. Not after he got my guard down, completely obliterated it. Not after, he all but ordered me to take care of Tami, so he could go to the lunch meeting without me.

Oh, my God. How stupid am I?

The room spins, and I have to hold onto the edge of the desk to keep myself upright. After everything, after all the time I worked to stay on my toes and sharp, I let a sharp suited salesman play me for a fool.

I allowed it in the end. He didn't even have to try very hard.

I can't breathe. Tears choke me. I have to see Rodney. I have to tell him what happened. This cannot stand. It must not. I was ready to be mature and not bring the boss into it, but I can't now. Not when he's taken advantage of me this way.

I should have trusted my gut instinct.

With my fists clenched, I walk in sharp, quick strides toward Rodney's office. What's he going to think when I tell him the truth? His golden boy won't look so golden anymore. It'll ruin Rodney's opinion of me and my reputation at the office, but there's no way I'm going to let him get away with this. Maybe I won't tell him about last night, but I'll give him enough information that he'll know for sure what a louse Zack is. A liar and a pig. Just like I always knew he was.

There Rodney is, inside his glass-walled office with Zack.

And a bottle of champagne, which he's just opening.

And two glasses. Zack is holding one of them out to be filled as he laughs.

Oh, my God. *E tu* Rodney! I think I'm going to throw up. The two of them, celebrating like this, while I stand here and watch them. I don't know what to do. I want to scream, I want to curse them both out, I want to throw things, break things, and rave like a lunatic because everything is falling apart. Everyone lied to me and used me. I was never going to get the sale.

I was never going to get the man.

My eyes fill with tears as I run to get my purse from my desk. I have to get out of here. Forget this place, forget Zack and Rodney and everything else. I don't ever want to see either of them again.

I run for the elevator, bumping into a pair of girls walking with their backs to me. They show surprise and concern, but I ignore them. They don't matter. Nothing matters as much as getting out of here does.

"Sienna!" Zack's voice is behind me, as I jam my finger against the button. I should've taken the stairs. I turn blindly in the direction of the stairwell as a heavy hand falls on my shoulder.

The bastard. He thinks he can touch me. I whirl around and barely have time to confirm that it is, indeed, Zack before my right hand swings and makes stinging contact with his cheek.

He steps back, raising his hand to his cheek in surprise. I see the white imprint of his fingers and palm. "What's that for?" he asks, his eyes wide.

"As if you didn't know. Shouldn't you be in Rodney's office, celebrating the sale you made without me? Go ahead. I don't want to interrupt your celebration. Enjoy it. I hope you choke on it." I'm so furious, so broken hearted, I can hardly speak. But he needs to know. He chose to follow me, so he needs to know that I know.

"What are you talking about?" he demands, his hand falling to his side.

"How can you lie like this?" I shout, and I don't care anymore who hears. I don't care what they think. I'm tired of cultivating an image of polished professionalism, of holding myself above them. I'm clearly no better than anyone in this place if it was so easy for a man to lie and use me the way he did. "You signed with the Dawsons yesterday, huh? And only your name is on the contract! I saw you in there with your champagne, celebrating your success. What excuse did you give Rodney, huh? For me not being part of it?"

He sighs, his shoulders slumping.

Yes, I got him. I called him out. And now he can't handle it.

"Come with me," he mutters, taking me by the wrist.

"Get your filthy, lying, piggy hands off me. I'm not going anywhere with you!"

"I said, come with me." He's not taking no for an answer as he clamps his hand over my arm and drags me down the hall toward his cubicle at the other end.

I feel the eyes of all my workmates on me the whole way there. I hear whispers and giggles and I want to burn the whole place down. I hope this is nice entertainment for them.

When we reach the cubicle, he closes the door before reaching into a drawer. "I made a mistake yesterday and I didn't notice it until this morning. I already called them to apologize and let them know I need them to sign another version of the document. Believe me, I feel like the least professional person in the world right now."

"Yeah, right," I snarl. "Why did you have that version with only your name on it?"

"Because I'm an ass," he hisses, shoving another contract at me. "That's the real one. I took the wrong one by mistake, the one I put only my name on, last week when we were both trying to take the sale from each other. Don't pretend you weren't thinking along the same lines. I wasn't paying attention when I took it to the restaurant."

When I look down at the contract he is holding out, it seems his story is legit. This version bears both our names.

"Call them yourself, if you want. They'll tell you I already spoke with them and I was going to drive over to their house this morning to make things right."

"I wouldn't do that anyway, and you know it," I point out, handing the contract back. "It looks like we're not on the same page."

"Regardless, you can come with me if you want to. You'll see that everything's on the up and up." He shrugs, hands spread. "What else can I say? I was selfish when I drew up that original version. That was before, before... I didn't know you then. I was only looking out for myself. I was determined to prove myself and be the big hero. I realize I was wrong."

I want to believe him. Dear God, forgive me for being a fool. I want to believe him. "What? What was the champagne for, then? Why didn't you invite me in to celebrate with you?"

He grimaces, his eyes leaving mine. "That had nothing to do with the sale of the house."

"Oh. I'm sorry. The two of you break out a bottle of bubbly every morning around this time?" I ask, hands on my hips. "I know you haven't closed on any other houses, since this is the only listing you're working on at the moment."

He looks uncomfortable, and for a moment, I think he's going to tell me to mind my own business. Then he tells me, "That's about something nobody knows about but Rodney and me. I wanted it that way. I didn't want to ruin anything."

My eyes narrow suspiciously. "Ruin what?"

"I guess it's safe for me to tell you now." He perches on the edge of the desk.

For a second, I have to fight off the urge to laugh. What is he, a spy? Will he have to kill me once I know the truth about his identity or something?

"Today marks the end of my apprenticeship," he explains with a sheepish grin.

I feel my face scrunching up into a scowl. "An apprentice?"

"Like I said, I didn't want anyone to know. I didn't want people kissing my ass or treating me different because of who I am."

I stare at him dumbfounded. "Why? Who you are?"

"I had an agreement with the owner of the agency, Rodney's boss, in other words. The man who owns the entire chain of offices, from coast to coast. He's retiring at the end of the year, and he needs a replacement. At the end of my apprenticeship, if I was successful and had put up solid numbers, I would be named his successor. I knew I could have sold this listing on my own, and I needed to prove to him that I was the man for the job. Do you understand why I did what I did now?"

Once again, I need to hold onto the desk to keep myself

upright. "Wait a second. You're telling me you're going to run the entire company?"

He nods. "In my father's place. Yes."

"Your father? You're Zack Dunhurst?" I whisper, my mouth falling open.

"Yes." He laughs at my expression.

I frown. "So Parker is not your name?"

"It's my mother's last name, but like I said, I didn't want word getting around that I was the boss's son. I wanted to be just like everyone else. Rodney was just congratulating me on the completion of a successful apprenticeship. I was going to ask you to dinner again tonight and come clean about the entire thing. I didn't expect you to see us and come to the wrong conclusion."

And again, the world is spinning around me. Not because I've been betrayed this time, but because I was so wrong —all along.

"Sienna." He reaches for me, and I go to him without thinking twice, allowing him to take my arms in his hands and pull me closer. "I know this is going to sound insane after all the dirty tricks I pulled on you, but I'm fucking crazy about you."

"You are?"

"I am. Now that it's all over and I can be honest about who I really am, I want to be honest about everything. So I thought you should know."

A smile—wide and disbelieving—spreads over my face. It only makes sense, him and me. The parts of our personalities that made us such good enemies make us even better partners. He's everything I've ever looked for. He gets me, he understands my ambition, he respects my work ethic and celebrates my successes.

Not to mention the fact that he motivates me to do better.

And he turns me on without having to try.

"You drive me crazy," I whisper, stroking his jaw with my fingertips, "but that's probably because I'm crazy about you, too."

It looks like Tami was right, I think as he pulls me in for a long, lingering kiss that promises so much. She'll never let me live this down.

## SIENNA

ONE MONTH LATER...

Z ack laughs over the phone. "Take your panties off."

"Why?"

"Because I said so."

"Look, I'm not masturbating in my office, okay? It's completely inappropriate, besides anyone could come in."

"Lock the door and close the blinds."

"No," I protest. "It will look suspicious if I do."

"Don't worry I'll do it," he says as he opens my office door and walks in.

I stare at him open-mouthed as he starts closing the blinds. "Zack, what are you doing here?"

He turns towards me, a crooked smile on his lips. "What do you think I'm doing here?"

"No." I start shaking my head. "No, seriously. You can't just barge in here."

He rubs his chin. "I'm the boss. I can barge in anywhere."

I cross my hands over my chest. I can never resist him when his eyes twinkle like that. "I'll have to report this as a sexual harassment incident."

He grins. "Go ahead, report me to anyone you want, but now will you please take those fucking panties off, babe. I've only got a few minutes between meetings."

"What if they hear us? These walls are paper-thin."

He takes a step towards me. "I want them to. I want everyone to know you're my woman."

Giddy with excitement and feeling incredibly horny, I stand up and quickly get out of my panties. They're already soaking.

He beckons me with his fingers and I walk around the desk to him. He's already unzipping his trousers and his cock is, as usual, hard as a tree trunk. I turn around and place my palms on the desk. He hitches my skirt up and over my hips and I back up on his bare cock. I moan as the thick shaft slides into my wetness. I keep on backing until it is all the way in.

"Oh God, I love your cock," I moan. No matter how many times he enters me, I never stop feeling awe at how truly massive he is, how full he makes me feel.

"Fuck yourself, babe," he growls, as he stuffs my panties into my mouth. I did not see him pick them up from the table.

I begin slowly, luxuriating in the sensation of his dick stretching me, before I really fuck myself on his hard length. The excitement of knowing we're doing it in my office made my orgasm build with shocking speed. As I get ready to climax he begins pumping too, making me feel as if the whole desk is shaking. I bounce back and he pumps forward until I scream. My cry is muffled, but hell—it's certainly not quiet. But I have no time to think of that as one of the most intense orgasms of my life cascades through me. I freeze, my muscles contracting and locking, as he keeps pounding away, hard, fast and deep into me. It makes the pleasure last long after the initial intensity of my orgasm passes.

When I feel his thighs start to harden against the backs of my legs, I know he too, is about to climax. I whip my panties out of my mouth and quickly whirl around. Dropping to my knees, I take his cock in my mouth. It didn't take me long to learn how to deep throat him. He slides deep into my throat, and I taste my own juices on his cock as I milk it by sucking him hard.

With an involuntary grunt, he shoots his cum directly down my eager throat.

I hold onto his hips and give his cock a lavish, meticulous suck before I stand up.

Zack grasps my face in his hands and kisses me deep and long. "I'll say it again. Nobody does it quite like you. You are perfect, Sienna. Just perfect," he whispers.

I grin softly. "Yeah, and I'll say it again. I've never met anybody with a cock like yours. It's quite, quite delicious."

He laughs and starts to put his clothes right. "Got to run, but I'll see you tonight."

"Tonight," I whisper.

"Don't put your panties back on. I want to think of you going around the office bare."

I giggle. "Okay."

# EPILOGUE

## SIENNA

*One Year Later*

"Tell him we won't go below eight-fifty," I bark into the phone as I stride off the elevator, nodding to everyone I pass along the way to my office. Rodney is at the desk in his office, kitty-corner from mine, and I wave as I pass by.

"Everything okay?" Denise asks as I end the call. She is waiting in the chair across from my desk with a notepad in hand. We've been together for eight months and I have to admit, I wonder why it took me so long to ask for an assistant. She's a gem, and it's so much easier to get my work done when she's taking care of the administrative duties.

"Oh, sure. The Becketts' lawyer, trying to lowball us. I know they'll settle on eight-fifty."

"The owner will be happy." She grins as I take a seat opposite hers.

I grin back, unable to contain my pride. "They spent just over six-hundred on it. They'll sing our praises."

Once we're finished with our early morning catch-up, she closes the door behind her and allows me a little privacy. I was so right to pressure Rodney into building me an office of my own. The leverage I had after selling Nick's house last year helped quite a bit. As I told him, an agent who sells multi-million-dollar estates shouldn't be working in a cubicle.

I should've asked sooner because he agreed immediately.

My phone rings as I'm finishing going through my inbox, and I can't keep the smile from my face as I answer in a low, seductive voice. "Yes? But make it quick. I'm a very busy woman, you know."

"I intend to make you even busier tonight," Zack purrs.

The man can make my toes curl even over the phone. "Oh? What did you have in mind, sir?"

"I don't know. Dinner, maybe? At home?"

"Ooh, an intimate evening. I like the sound of that."

"You think so?"

"I know so." I grin, dropping the act. "Only if you're cooking, though. No fair asking me over only to have me cook."

He laughs. "I was going to suggest we order in."

"Even better. No offense, but you need to expand your repertoire a little."

"Gee, thanks. You've never complained about my performance in the kitchen before now."

I blush, pressing my lips together before replying, "I was talking about what you do at the stove, not what you do on top of the island."

He growls softly. "And the counter, and the floor, and…"

"Zack," I warn, as I start to squirm in my chair.

He laughs. "See you at seven."

---

"Can I tell you a secret?"

Zack looks up at me, chopsticks in the air. "What's that?"

"I like nights like this even better than the times when we go out on the town. This is so much more my speed." I pull my feet up onto the sofa. I'm dressed in the sweats I keep in his dresser and my hair up in a bun on top of my head.

"You mean, you don't like it when I wine and dine you? I wish I had known. I could've saved a lot of money this last year."

I poke at him with my chopsticks.

Sparring a bit with me, he deftly defends himself.

I roll my eyes. "Ha, ha. You know what I mean."

He leans back, feet up on the coffee table. "I do. You know I feel the same way. I've always been more of a homebody."

Just another way in which we're perfect for each other. I figured out quite some time ago that all the time I spent telling myself I hated him was a waste. He's my match in every way.

Including at work, where he maintains a desk at Rodney's branch and comes in every so often to work with me on a complicated sale. We've managed to put together a half-dozen deals like the one we did last year, the selling price higher and higher every time. He's allowed me to up my game in every way, both with him and on my own.

"Oh, you know what? I left a bottle of wine in the fridge. Can you grab it for me?" He smiles at me.

"What's wrong with your legs?" I ask, looking pointedly at them. "Did they break all of a sudden?"

He sighs. "Come on. I've had a long day, and I would like to relax in my own home for a little bit. Is it so much to ask my woman get a bottle of wine for me? I'd do it for you."

"Right I'll do it for you, but watch it with the 'my woman' crap," I mutter as I get up. His chuckle follows me into the kitchen as I take the bottle of Chablis out, uncork it, and pick out a pair of glasses before heading back to the living room.

"Thanks. I'll pour," he offers.

"You're such a gentleman." I smile, handing the glasses over.

"You know, your charming personality is by far one of my favorite things about you."

When he hands me my glass, I notice the strange look in his eye. "What's up?"

"Hmm?"

"What's up? You look like there's something you want to tell me, but you don't know how to say it."

"How do you always manage to see through me?"

I shrug, grinning. "I've made a habit out of studying you over this year together, you know. You're practically a full-time job." I'm still chuckling as I lean forward to place the glass on the coffee table and pick up my container of fried rice.

And that's when I notice what he added to my meal. Or, more specifically, what's now hanging from the chopsticks I left in the container.

"What about signing a lifetime contract for that full-time job you just described?" he asks.

I pick up the container with a shaking hand, bringing it closer to my face so I can study the ring which seems to be almost as big as a cherry. "Is this for me?" I whisper, admiring the way the diamonds sparkle in the light from the TV.

"Who else could carry off a ring like that one?" he asks.

"The ring is one thing." I finally pry my eyes from it and focus on him.

He's kneeling in front of me now.

"It's what the ring means."

"The ring means I love you, and I want you to be my wife."

"Zack…"

He watches the emotions flicker over my face. "Marry me," he urges, his voice is thick with feeling.

I can't speak. My hands are shaking. I've never seen him quite like this.

He's always so cool and confident. Now he looks as if he's unsure. As if his very life depends on my answer. "Marry me, Sienna."

"Are you sure about this?" I whisper.

"I've never been more sure of anything in my life. You'll make me the happiest man alive by saying yes."

"Oh Zack," I say, and my voice breaks. Tears that have gathered without my knowledge slide down my face. I swallow the frog in my throat.

"You're supposed to be happy, you idiot."

Filled with overwhelming joy and happiness, I start to laugh.

He watches me for a second, then he too, starts to laugh. "Okay, now I'm starting to worry about your answer," he says.

My arms go around his neck and I rest my forehead against his. "Do you really love me, Zack?"

"I'm only going to say this once, because you know, street cred and everything. What I feel for you, Sienna cannot be described. Even love is too weak a word for it. I need you like I need air. I would kill for you. That would be too easy. I would die for you. I know I can live like this with you for eternity, but I want to claim you. I want you to be just mine. I want every man who looks at you to understand immediately that you belong to me. You're damn well taken. I want to see your belly grow big with our children. I want to hold you while your hair turns and your skin wrinkles. For better, for worse, through sickness and pain I want you by my side. I want everything with you, or nothing with anyone else. You are everything to me, Sienna. Everything." He pauses. "Now, for fuck's sake, will you marry me?"

I look into his beautiful eyes and my voice is hushed with the wonder of the moment. "I love you, Zack. Like I've loved no one."

I see the relief come into is eyes. He wasn't kidding. He really was worried I might say no.

I tangle my hands in his silky hair and pull his head down. The kiss is slow, deep and passionate.

"Can I take that as a yes?" he asks with a grin, when our lips part.

I laugh. "Yes, yes, yes, yes, a million times over," I shout.

He glances around. "This is not the most romantic of scenarios, but I just couldn't imagine waiting another minute. That ring has been burning a hole in my pocket all weekend. I just had to give it to you."

"Oh, Zack."

Everything goes blurry as he takes the container from me, sliding the ring up over the chopsticks. I can't believe I'm holding out my left hand for him to slide the most beautiful, perfect ring I've ever seen... over my finger.

He kisses the back of my hand.

Suddenly, I'm glad that we're not at the top of the Eiffel Tower, or the Empire State Building, or some other wonderful place with a terrific view, candles and flowers, that we're not both dressed to the nines and enjoying a gourmet meal. What matters is right now, the two of us, being together without anyone around to see what I am going to do next.

And that I love him more than I thought possible.

"Of course, I will," I whisper, and anything else I have to say is lost when he kisses me.

That's all right. I have the rest of my life to say everything that's in my heart.

And they lived happily ever after... :-)

# SWEET REVENGE (SAMPLE CHAPTERS)

# CHAPTER 1

## DAWN

"Wait. What? Are you…dumping me?" I gasp in disbelief, as I lean back against the cupboard to steady myself.

"I guess so," he mutters, his shifty eyes sliding away.

"I guess so? What the hell does that mean? Are you, or aren't you?" I demand incredulously.

His sullen face swings back to me. His fists are clenched by his sides as though he's forcing himself to sit there and not bolt out of the front door. "All right, yes. Yes, I am."

"That's it? It's over between us," I say in wonder, just in case there is any doubt. It's always good to be completely clear about these things. When someone says all right yes. It's kind of a grudging agreement. It could mean no too.

He rolls his eyes. I hate when he does that. It makes him look like a dork. "That would be a safe assumption to make," he says, with a little snigger. He's loving this. This position of power. He told me that he's never been the one doing the dumping before. Every woman he's been with was smart enough to leave him first.

I shake my head as my brain tries to make sense of the thoughts flying through my head.

James and I have been together for two years. In fact, only two months ago he told me he was so grateful he had found me. We were perfectly matched and there would never be anyone else for him. However, our anniversary last week was kind of a mess. I somehow, convinced myself he was going to propose. Well, what would you think if you saw a bridal magazine stuffed under his pillow in his apartment?

When he didn't pop the question, and came up with the lame suggestion we get chicken take-out and just hang out at my apartment for the evening, I was pretty gutted. But I'm not one to give up at the drop of a hat and I decided to somehow salvage the night. I slipped into some expensive lingerie and swayed towards the bed in what he used to call my sexy walk, but he turned out the lights and fucked me for five minutes. It could have been longer, but it felt like less.

Not exactly the romantic night of my dreams. I had half a mind to flip on my vibrator and masturbate right there in front of him, but he started snoring next to me. Since I wasn't turned on anyway, there seemed to be no real point.

I stare at him now. "But it's New Year's Eve tomorrow."

He has the grace to look shamefaced.

"Why?" I whisper.

"Does it matter?" he snaps, flying upright and crossing his arms. Like a child who has been naughty and doesn't want to be told off. I'm so used to dealing with his tantrums and moods that I automatically reach out to comfort him, to make it all better even though he's a grown-ass man, and I'm the injured party here.

He evades my touch as if it is a branch of poison ivy and moves out of reach. My hand falls back heavily against my thigh. The slapping sound reverberates inside my skull. Wow! He can't even bear my touch. Okkkkkay. I take a deep breath and measure out my words slowly, clearly. "Yes, it does matter. I'd really like to know."

He snorts. "What difference does it make?"

I swallow the pure rage stuck in my throat. This asshole thinks he can walk in here and break up with me after he's wasted two whole years of my time, and not even give me a reason. I don't know what gave him that impression because I'm absolutely determined to find out why. Heck, I'll sit on his spineless back and squeeze it out of him if I have to. I straighten away from the cupboard. "Since it makes no difference to you, and as you don't have anything to lose," I point out through gritted teeth, "perhaps you will be kind enough to tell me what the *fuck* is going on here."

He turns back to me slowly, looking me dead in the eye, a nasty expression in his eyes.

Suddenly, I know what this is about. When he arrived early this evening, I think I already knew what was coming my way. Especially, when he sat on the edge of the couch without taking his shoes or coat off. He had no intention of hanging around too long. He wanted to get in and out. Some confident part of me wishes that I could back out of hearing him say it. I would love to airily walk him to the front door, while telling him to keep his pathetic reasons and fuck off out of my life, I'm just not interested to know.

But I can't do that.

I'm someone who needs to know. I need closure. If I don't get it out of him now I'll be calling him in a month or six months and asking him why then. So I'll be damned if I don't get him to spit it now. I square my shoulders. I'm a big girl. I can take it. Besides, I refuse to give him the satisfaction of thinking he crushed me like a bug under his shoe. After two years that's not how I'm going to let this end. Me splattered under his clumsy big left foot. Actually, for a man with such big feet he has a very small dick.

"You really want to know?" There's that ugly look again.

I nod.

He tosses his hands in the air in exasperation. "Just remember *you* wanted to go down this road."

"Just, spit it out, James," I growl.

"I met someone else, all right."

# CHAPTER 2

## DAWN

I was expecting it, but my stomach still drops. I look down at the ground in front of me. Yeah, I knew in my gut he'd been pulling away from me. I even briefly wondered if it had something to do with the new girl at his work he kept talking about. The girl with the lap-dancer name, but of course, I convinced myself that he was not that type of guy. He was faithful. He was in love with me.

"The slut at work?"

He flushes a deep red. "There is no need to get judgmental."

"Is it?" I demand, my anger boiling over.

"As a matter of fact, yes. Her name is Candy and she's not a slut. She's a great gal. She has a really lovely personality. She's always helping everyone."

My eyes widen. What is this fool doing now? He'll be telling me she's great in bed next.

"The first time we had sex," he confesses enthusiastically.

"She went down on me an…fuck, Dawn, she blew my mind. It was so much hotter than anything we ever had together."

I feel as though I am going to throw up. I press my lips together determined not to show myself up. Anyway, vomit is murder to get out of cream carpets. He notices the horror in my face and resolves to rub it in, for reasons that I can't quite figure out.

"I guess it's because she's hotter than you," he continues, getting into it now, apparently reveling in the power he has over me, the power to devastate me. "She's at least fifty pounds lighter than you…"

I can't help wincing as those words come out of his mouth. I can't believe he would say that to me. He knows how self-conscious I am about the way I look, and yet he can't resist twisting the knife deep into the most painful of my insecurities. This is starting to feel like revenge. He doesn't love me He hates me. An image of this woman pops into my head. She's slim and tiny and cute, and next to her I am a great heaving mound of flesh. And he *wants* to have sex with her… with the lights on. For more than five minutes.

I wonder how long he's been sitting on all of this, how many times he'd wanted nothing more than to tear me apart this way. I should just kick him out. And yet, I don't. Not yet, anyway.

"What about our tickets for tomorrow night?" They cost an arm and a leg.

"Uh, I thought since you probably won't want to go on your own anyway, I'll just take Candy."

I shake my head in wonder. What a bag of shit he turned out

to be. I paid for half of those tickets. My brain shifts gear. I never knew him. Now I need to know if I should get tested for anything. "How long has your affair been going on?"

"A month or so," he replies, and looks at me so brazenly, I wonder if he is even a little bit ashamed. Knowing he cares so little, that he's so happy to rub all this in my face, sends a flare of fury through my system. I'm not going to let him walk all over me like this. To be honest this man has been nothing but a burden for the last two years. I've done everything I could for him. I put his interest before mine, and now he's standing in front of me telling me he's betrayed me, and instead of being apologetic, he actually sounds victorious and proud of himself.

I know for damn sure that if he was cheating on me he wouldn't have used protection if he could avoid it. That's just the kind of guy he is. I guess I had always seen it, but now that it's laid out in front of me, so inescapably and utterly ugly, I have no choice but to accept that and try to protect myself as best I can.

"Did you use protection?"

He swallows hard. "No, but she's clean-"

"You're such a fucking piece of shit," I shout, rounding on him. Any sadness and hurt in my heart is replaced with burning fury. "Clean? How clean can she be if she didn't use a condom with you?"

"You're just jealous," he says smugly, and I think I see the hint of a smile on his face and it makes me so angry I actually want to scratch his lying eyes out.

"What is there to be jealous about?" I fire back, my voice

lifting in volume. I don't want this to become a yelling match, but if he's going to keep being such a prick...

He frowns, as though caught off guard, and I decide to go in for the kill just the same way he did for me when he told me how much slimmer this new girlfriend of his happens to be.

"You're a cheater," I begin, lifting my fingers and ticking off all his flaws one by one. "You're so cheap you used to make me cringe. You're rude to waiters. You snore worse than a pig. This new girl is welcome to you. Though maybe I should call her up first and let her know what she's getting herself into? Oh, and I nearly forgot. You're garbage in bed." There's a twist of triumph to my voice as I finish up all the ways that he's failed me over the last two years, all the ways he's been a shitty boyfriend to me.

His jaw drops.

I know I've hit a nerve, and it feels good for a moment, but I'm not a cruel person at heart and any kind of joy I might have gotten from seeing him so upset soon becomes a sour taste in my mouth and I find myself staring at him with more sadness than anything else. I should tear the shit out of him, and God knows that he deserves it, but for whatever reason it's just not fun right now.

I'm too hurt by his betrayal to really find any kind of consolation in the way he looks right now. I wish I could be a little more callous and cold and really go at him, chip away at his ego the way he's done with mine for more than a year now, but I can't. I'm just exhausted, and what I want more than anything in the world is for him to get the hell out of my apartment so I never have to see him again.

"If I was garbage in bed it was because I had a lump of whale meat in bed with me. Who can get turned on by that?" he yells.

"I hope I never see you again," I say slowly, and I really mean it too.

He opens his mouth to speak, but I've had enough. "You should leave," I point to the door, leaving no room for discussion.

"With pleasure," he sneers. Turning for the door, he walks out, and slams it so hard the walls rattle.

I close my eyes to quell the next wave of anger that overtakes me. I just want to run out there and scream at him for being such an asshole. The kind of idiot who seriously believes that slamming someone's door at this time of the night was a good way to make a statement.

What a fucking jerk.

# CHAPTER 3

I stand frozen, listening to his footsteps echo down the corridor. As soon as the entrance door of my apartment building closes, I find myself sinking into the couch. I stare blankly into space.

So this is what it feels like to be dumped. Well, I have been dumped before, but never by someone I've been with for so long, and not for another woman.

To my surprise there is more anger than heartbreak pulsing through my veins. Maybe the sadness will come later, but for now, all I can feel is a deep sense of betrayal. I trusted him. I thought we were both society's rejects who had found each other. Nobody wanted me and nobody wanted him and we had found a way to be good together. We once talked about making children. That was the first time I agreed to do it with him without a condom. I frown. Was he manipulating me even then? Because he never spoke about kids again after that.

God, how much time I've wasted on him.

My mind drifts back to when we first met. I was fresh out of college and had just started the internship that would one day become my full-time job. I was so confident, so passionate, so ambitious, and then I ran into this guy who had seemed so perfect for me. I was in advertising, he was in marketing. I actually saw us as a power couple. What a laugh. Thinking back now, I can see clearly that we were only a perfect couple for the first few months. After that all those subtle comments started. About my looks in general, my unfeminine laugh, but mostly my weight. All the little jokes. Once when we were going on vacation, he joked with the airline staff to seat someone equally heavy on the other side of the plane so that I didn't tilt the plane, and make it fly lopsided.

Slowly, with every strike he chiseled away at my confidence. Over time I no longer felt like a full-blown raging fire, I hated it, but I was slowly but surely being turned down to a fickle flame of my former self. I can still remember how it felt to be so full of light and energy, even if I can't muster up a drop of it for myself at this very moment.

I sit forward.

No, I'm not going to sit here feeling sorry for myself, and hope that somehow my life is going to get itself back on track. I'll do something about this. It's scary as hell, looking out on a life you never thought you'd face, but I can handle it. I can be single again. Maybe the lap dancer did me a favour when she went down on him.

I force myself to my feet and sway with the strong emotions running through my body.

Ignoring the voice in my head that seems intent on repeating the cruel words, specifically, about how much lighter his new girlfriend is than me, I begin to pace the floor of my apartment. I try to focus my mind on one thing at a time.

But those negative words nag at the back of my head. I have to address them.

What did I expect? I was making him feeling guilty and he needed an excuse. Attack is the best form of defense, and he knew exactly where to stick the knife to make sure that I'd bleed for hours afterwards. My weight is a sore point for me.

I've always been a buxom gal, but while I was with him I just couldn't stop the weight from piling on. To be fair it was partly his fault. I'd always stopped eating before seven, but he liked to eat late so he would often order fried chicken, or pizza late at night. He would have a couple of pieces, then he would force me to finish it, because he would make me feel as if wasting the food would somehow impact the starving children in Africa.

But now that I think about it. He was funny about my weight even when we first got together and I was still full of lovely curves, he never really paid me any compliments, or was positive about the way I looked. He preferred to make love with the lights off and it would often feel like he was trying to touch as little of my body as possible. The sex wasn't awful at the start, when the two of us were still getting to know each other, our likes and dislikes, but in the last six months it's been terrible.

I tried everything I could to switch things up, doing whatever I could in the vain hope that it might turn him on or get him to do more than roll on top of me, thrust for a few minutes, and then roll off. Oh, and of course he always loved his blowjobs. Those he had as regular as clockwork. Three sometimes four times a week. To the point, I felt that was all I was good for.

Filling my belly with his slightly bitter cum.

He would lay there with his eyes shut, groaning, "oh baby yes, yes, just like that," while I worked on him. I tried to pretend he was encouraging me, but I knew in my heart he was imagining some other woman. A woman he was actually attracted to. A thinner, sexier woman. One of those women I had caught him looking at. Women who weren't anything like me.

I guess even that should have been enough, over the last two years, to completely crush my self-esteem. I look down at my body now, in a pair of jeans and a sweatshirt, and run my hands over it. I don't like what I feel. The lumps and bumps. They were not there before I started eating his leftover pizzas and chicken.

I know I want to change, to forge a new life for myself. But his words are still ringing in my ears, along with every barbed comment he's made to me about the way I look. The comparisons to his friend's girlfriends, leaving pictures of slim, toned women on his computer, buying me clothes a few sizes too small for my birthday because he wanted to give me something to work towards.

But I can do this for myself.

That's what I have to keep reminding myself. If I want, I can lose this weight and get in shape. I know my thighs will never touch unless I starve myself, but I don't actually want that. I just want to be a size where I can be happy and feel beautiful.

I'll start again. I'll go out there and just be me for a while. Eat when I want to, have great sex with a man who actually thinks I'm attractive, and control my own television's remote. It'll be great not to be putting down the toilet seat every time I want to pee and cleaning urine off the floor every damn day. I won't have to hear his relentless disapproving voice every single time I do anything that he doesn't like, and quite frankly, that has become almost everything I do. God, the other day, he was complaining about the way I breathe. I can just do one load of washing a week instead of three. I won't have to suck his small cock again.

Yes, enough of being a doormat.

As I pace up and down the apartment, a smile forms on my face. I don't want to do this for revenge. I don't want to do this for him. No, in fact, if he had been a little kinder to me about all of this over the course of our relationship maybe I'd have been more inclined to do something about it before now. I stop pacing suddenly. I never thought about it before, but every time I so much as hinted that I was thinking about losing weight, he did everything in his power to covertly and subtly sabotage me. He brought sweets into the house, he ordered even more take-out at night and he made plans for us to go out for dinner when he knew I was planning on hitting the gym. Or he would suddenly want to cuddle on the couch with a movie.

So, I'm not going to do this to spite him. I'm going to do this in spite of him. Not because I want him back, or because I want him to regret his decision. No, I can't imagine any time soon where I'd want James back in my life. Candy is welcome to him. I just want to be happy with my body again, to prove to myself that the driven, passionate woman who had existed before James smothered her in fat is still buried inside me somewhere.

I'll start tonight. Right now.


Out Soon...

## CONNECT WITH RIVER

To receive special offers, contests opportunities, bonus content, info on new releases, and great deals from other authors sign up for River's newsletter.

Email me at:
riverlaurent1@gmail.com
Or come say hello here:

33722205R00144

Printed in Great Britain
by Amazon